THE

COUSINS' COURTSHIP.

BY JOHN R. WISE.

IN TWO VOLUMES.

VOL. II.

1859.

British Library Cataloguing-in-Publication Data
A catalogue record for this book is available from the
British Library

John Richard de Capel Wise

John Rickard de Capel Wise was born on 1st April 1831, as the eldest son of John Robert Wise (a former British consul-general in Sweden) and his wife Jane. He attended Grantham Grammar School in the market town of Grantham, Lincolnshire, England – and subsequently enrolled at the University of Oxford. He began his studies in 1849, at Lincoln College, but took no degree, and left the university to travel abroad.

On returning to England he wandered through many country districts, frequently changing his residence. Wise held radical views on religion and politics, and according to his friend, Walter Crane (a celebrated artist and illustrator), Wise had been intended for the Church – but left Oxford due to his theological disagreements. Wise also quarrelled with his parents, apparently 'on account of his free opinions.' During the course of his wanderings, he came to know John Chapman, the editor of the *Westminster Review.* As a result of this friendship, for many years he wrote the section on *Belles-Lettres* in that magazine, but withdrew suddenly owing to political differences with Chapman. His relations with the *Westminster* also brought him the acquaintance of George Henry Lewes and George Eliot.

After this, Wise contributed to the *Reader,* a weekly periodical which advanced political views as radical as Wise's own. He was also a correspondent for a London paper during the Franco-Prussian War in 1870. Wise never married, but enjoyed a prolific career in writing. His first work was a pamphlet of poems called *Robin Hood* published in 1855. In 1860 he issued a novel in two volumes called *The Cousin's Courtship* with little success. Following repeated visits to Stratford-upon-Avon he published (1861) a volume on *Shakespeare: his Birthplace and its Neighbourhood*. The book contained a description of the local scenery, the natural history, the literary associations and dialect of Stratford-upon-Avon.

He lived in the New Forest (in southern England) in the early 1860s, which allowed him to research and write his book on the locality, but by the summer of 1863 he was residing in lodgings near Hathersage in the Peak District. This book was *The New Forest: its History and its Scenery* (1862), by far his most popular work, and it contained sixty-two illustrations drawn by Walter Crane and engraved by William James Linton. The most sought after edition by collectors was the 'artist's edition' of 1883, to which Heywood Sumner added twelve etchings, and which had Linton's woodcuts mounted on India paper.

Wise had hoped to write a book on the Peak District, similar to the one he had written for the New Forest but did not receive sufficient encouragement to go on with the work. By 1875 he was settled at Sandsend, but soon after migrated to Edwinstowe, Nottinghamshire. In 1881 he anonymously published an elaborate volume called *The First of May: A Fairy Masque,* which he dedicated to Charles Darwin. It was also illustrated by Walter Crane, but was financially unsuccessful. Wise re-visited Lyndhyrst in the New Forest in August 1889, and stayed there throughout the winter.

Wise was in poor health however, and his winter trip to the forest did him no good. He died the following spring, on 1st April 1890, aged fifty-nine, and was buried in Lyndhurst Cemetery.

CONTENTS

OF THE SECOND VOLUME.

THE COUSINS' COURTSHIP.

CHAPTER I.

A RIDE ON AN ENGINE.

BUT we must turn to other subjects. Reginald had heard several times at College from Miss Garland. She wrote in good spirits. He had sent her—against her wish, it should be added —some remittances every now and then, for he felt bound to protect her. Colonel Ancaster had written to him once or twice; " you will pleased to give me an account of yourself, as I still consider myself, notwithstanding the altered circumstances, your guardian," was the concluding sentence of each note; but it was meant kindly. Mrs. Neville, Minnie, and Florence, were all excellent correspondents; but he never heard from Aston. Men were now going down for the Christmas vacation.

Reginald had been again invited, thanks to Mrs. Neville, to Bushwood; and he determined again to go round by London. He wished, though, to take with him a present for Miss Garland. His fifty pounds at Clover's had long since dwindled down to a small sum, and he drew out the balance, which would but little more than pay for his travelling expenses. Leaming and Ermine, however, will be very glad to let him have a dress, or a cloak, or a muff, or a boa, or all of them, if he likes, on credit. Reginald cannot refuse the temptation, for poor Miss Garland he knows must need something this cold weather. The things are packed up, and he is soon off. The fields are covered with snow all along the line; but when he gets into London it looks as if the clouds had been snowing soot-flakes. The butchers' shops gleam a mass of scarlet. At the grocer's, holly and yew sprigs are sprouting in beds of currants and gardens of soft brown sugar. At the corners of the streets there are little snow maelstroms.

Past the 'buses with their freights of cold clerks sitting on the top, Reginald drives; past coroneted carriages with the fat coachman, and the footman looking like the coachman cut in half; past warmly muffled ladies carrying, as it were, so many skye terriers and cats in their hands, but which are only the fashionable hairy muffs of the day; past the poor wretched women who stand at public-houses, as if they expected to receive some warmth every time the door swung to and fro ; past shoeless, stockingless, hatless boys, looking in at a cookshop, where the steam is blowing off; past pyramids of oranges, and smooth white obelisks of sugar in grocers' shops.

At last Reginald reaches Islington. He jumps out; the wind is too keen to bargain with cabby about his fare. He runs up-stairs. There is poor Miss Garland sitting by a scanty fire sewing a shirt. Her poor fingers are cold, but still she sews. She has sewn through the summer, she has sewn through the autumn, but there is no harvest. Yes, there is a harvest, and she has reaped it. Her garner is full of care and sickness. Hers is a harvest of blood-shot eyes, of pale cheeks and aching brows, of the headache and the heartache. Reginald felt glad he had bought the dress, and boa, and muff, for the poor thing still wears her light summer dress this cold day.

"Wait a minute, Miss Garland, whilst I run down-stairs and bring up my present for you," which he soon did; "you must go and put them on, whilst I order dinner somewhere;" and when he came back he found her looking comfortable and warm. The dress fitted very well, and her little hands slipped into the warm little brown pillow of a muff, as if they had gone to sleep. Dinner soon arrives, for it is much too cold to walk out. But Miss Garland is altered. She was looking ill in the autumn, but she is looking worse now. This state of things cannot last much longer.

"Promise me you will do no more work at present, Miss Garland," said Reginald; but she was obstinate, and he could extract no promise from her, except some very vague assertions.

They talked about college and college life, but Reginald had little time to stay, for he promised Mrs. Neville to be at Bushwood the next day, and consequently must leave London by the night train.

"But I must go too; it is near my time," said Miss Garland.

Reginald did not exactly know what she meant. She laughed, and merely said, "It is close upon the hour."

"You are not going out such an evening as this?"

"Indeed I am; I would not miss my appointment for any consideration."

Reginald was puzzled, but had no time to make any further inquiries, or he would miss the train.

"Good bye, it is the last time you will ever see me"—he thought she said; "but I must be mistaken," he said to himself. She would not take a cab, and did not want any money. He was puzzled.

It was now dark; but Reginald could discern the gleaming flakes falling like sparks as the train rushes along. The train travels faster and faster, yet is behind time at all the stations. The snow, you would almost think, has choked the whistle up, so faintly it sounds. So at Gryndon another brazen-hoofed steed is harnessed to the long train, and away it starts again with its load of Christmas presents. Guards peep in at odd times and places, but the snow chokes up their lanterns. Reginald is looking out at some station where they have stopped.

"How do you do, Neville, eh?" It is Lord Cokeborough, and the officials all bow to him. He is going down to Bushwood. "Very heavy snow-storm. They are running tandem in front; two iron grays."

"I should so much like a mount, can you manage it for me?" said Reginald.

"Oh, I dare say I can; but I don't care much about that sort of thing myself." It is worth noticing how very little interest gentlemen who deal in shares take in engines. "There's only one man I know fond of engine-driving, and that's young Bare; he knows every engine in the Coke and Foco stables, as he calls the engine manufactory; how much weight it is up to, and all the feats it has performed. Stromboli is, I believe, his favourite animal: Stromboli out of Stephenson and Son; he has offered to back Stromboli against all the world." So at the next station, by Lord Cokeborough's influence, Reginald found himself standing on the first engine with the stoker and engineer, who, from the effects of the smoke and snow, looked like two negroes partially chalked over. "It's an odd taste that, for riding on an engine on a cold night," said Lord Cokeborough to himself, as he settled down again in the soft-padded, well-lighted, first-class carriage; "that young fellow, though, if I don't take care, will be before me with his cousin. Why, she will have at least sixty thousand pounds, besides half the Bushwood property." And his lordship fell back into a sweet reverie of sixty thousand pounds, mingled with happy dreams of railway scrip.

"It is as good as riding across country," said Reginald to himself, pleased with the excitement; the cold wind rushing against his face, and blowing his hair about. A complete foam of snow was rising up like a white cloud all round the buffers; the train, like a long white, supple-jointed snake with its brazen heads, swings round the curves. And now they are in a tunnel-mouth. Far away Reginald sees lights sparkling, which belong to the men working on the line, who hurry away as they hear the scream both engines give as they enter the darkness. The snow ceases to beat, but there is a smell of dampness, and mould, and foul air. The stoker opens the furnace-door, and the red light gleams along the sides of the walls, and reddens the great silver ice-stalactites which hang from the roof. The wheels slip, and whiz, and turn round fast in the air, as they miss their grip on the rails. The sand-boxes are full, and the sand is streaming out. They see ghost-figures crouching against the walls, and planks and "chairs," and bolts lying beside the rail; and then with a sudden crash again emerge into the snow-choked air, and dash past the rough-hewn stone of the cutting, so close, that Reginald almost dreads some projecting fragment would strike him. The line is now a dead level for miles; they thunder along by little roadside stations, throwing up a complete surf of snow in their rear, like the tail of some fiery comet. The air is now clearer, and the moon shines out for the first time; the snow down here has not covered the rails, which look like solid silver bars. The engines seem to bolt and gorge them down. The stoker is busy with his oil-can, feeding every bolt, and screw, and spring, from its long bill. The snow again comes down thicker than before, and hisses as it falls on the boiler; and when the stoker opens the fire-door, the flames dart out blue and sulphurous tongues, and when he jars it to, they still creep out. Slow coal trains pass; the coals looking like white diamonds instead of black— the great engines throb, and their brazen limbs sweat. Suddenly a sharp report as of a gun is heard. A wheel has gone. The engines rock from side to side, like a boat at sea. "Jump for your life," Reginald heard some one cry, and as he springs he feels the engine lurching,

as it were, from under him. He comes heavily
against the embankment, but is not much hurt.
At the same moment the carriages crash together
like so many tinder-boxes. The two great engines are lying along the rails; whilst their blue
and sulphur-coloured flames darting from the
stokeholes cast a fearful light, mingled with the
shrieks of the wounded and the hiss of the
steam.

"There's a goods train behind us," said the
engineer, who leaped off with Reginald, in alarm.

"Give me some fog signals, then," cried Reginald.

"By God, she is coming too," said the man,
laying his ear close to the rails.

Reginald started off as hard as he could run,
waving a red lantern. Down he rushed for some
six hundred yards. Over the fog signals came
the train, and pulled up just in time. A fire
was soon lighted with the broken carriages, and
the sufferers pulled out. A terrible wreck it was,
worse than any at sea; for there the merciful
waves drown the poor wretches at once. Regi-

nald worked all through that sad night, pulling the wounded out from under the mass of ruins.

"I hope Lord Cokeborough is all safe," said he to himself.

"I wonder whether Reginald Neville is killed," thought his lordship, for he had escaped unhurt, as an unlucky third-class carriage, as usual, acted as a buffer to the rest of the train.

CHAPTER II.

SKATING AND DANCING.

REGINALD had a long, sad tale to tell when he arrived at Bushwood the next day. Soon after Lord Cokeborough came; but his lordship is soon off to Mr. Aston Neville's study to talk about the railroad bills before committees in the House.

"He holds a time-table in his hand just as if it were a betting-book," said Minnie.

"Yes, but, my dear," answered Mrs. Neville, "he never holds a betting-book as if it were a time-table; for I am told that he is always behind time, like his father, in paying his debts."

"That comes from having so much to do with trains," Minnie replied.

, "Well, it is a great pity he should be so fond of the railway market, and I sincerely wish he would leave Aston alone. I hate this speculating and dabbling in railway shares."

"The stags do not any longer browse in Ironton Park, but in Ironton drawing-rooms," said Minnie; but Mrs. Neville looked very sad about the matter.

It is Christmas eve, and his lordship still stays on at Bushwood, and pays particular attention to Minnie. Little Flo is a good deal occupied with her governess, so Reginald does not see much of her. Mr. Aston Neville and his lordship sit long after dinner, and talk of other matters besides railways. Mrs. Neville and Minnie and Reginald have been out all day in the gardens gathering sprigs of yew and holly to ornament the house, for the gardeners cut such clumsy pieces. They wander out, too, in the deep woods. Still and silent is everything. The trees stand like brown corpses sheeted in white. The brook tinkles, as it knocks against the silver plates of ice which fringe its banks, and keeps chiming

and talking.   At last they discover the object of
their search.

" I am not so surprised that the Druids should
have paid such reverence to the mistletoe; it is
the only green thing in a world of frost and
barrenness," said Mrs. Neville.   " I fancy they
must have seen an emblem of future life in it.
How dead is the bark of the tree, and yet how
fresh are its leaves, and how its white berries
sparkle ! "

" A very pretty sentimental speech, mamma,"
replied Minnie, but Mrs. Neville had been un-
usually grave the last two or three days.

" Here is Alfred Craven and young Mr. Leighe
coming up the ride," said Minnie, so they came
forward to meet them.   Leighe was one of the
Craven set in St. Matthew's, and looked to Reginald always like a woman in man's clothes.

" We have come to ask you to act in some
private theatricals next Thursday," said Alfred
Craven.

" Well, it must be on condition that you come
over and help us with ours, for we are going

to have some again this year," replied Minnie, and so the matter was settled.

"Well," said Minnie, after Alfred Craven and his friend were gone, "if Mr. Leighe plays, as of course he will, in a lady's-maid's part, he will not want stays, so we need not order an extra pair for our theatre."

It was now late on Christmas eve. His lordship and Aston sat busy over their claret, discussing railway scrip.

"What can they be talking about all this time?" said Mrs. Neville.

Coffee had been several times announced to them, and at last came a message that they should not make their appearance in the drawing-room to-night. So the cousins sat by themselves. Frosty and cold was the night. The logs blazed merrily on the fire, as if gunpowder grew in their fibres, and thousands of sparks jetted out with sharp crackling reports. They had been talking about the two exquisites who had called to-day, and Reginald had been comparing them with Saber. The gallant Saber made various essays at athletic games, as the reader knows; but Leighe had never touched a bat, and would as soon think of taking up an adder. He has been frequently known to ask, with wonderful sarcasm, "Do you call that pleasure?" pointing to the St. Matthew's eight, when the men were putting on a spirt. He preferred being punted on the Cherwell. His galley, for punt we cannot call it, was gorgeously fitted; and in it upon a pile of soft cushions was this King of Sheba arrayed in all his glory.

"Why the deuce doesn't the wind turn over the pages of my book?" he thinks, as he reads the last fashionable novel; and the wind does turn over the pages of it for him; but since the south-west wind cannot read very well, it unfortunately turns two pages over at once; but the great king is far too idle to put the matter right, or perhaps he does not find out this slight mistake on the south-west wind's part, or perhaps the fashionable novel reads just as well, as far as the sense is concerned, with two pages turned over, instead of one.

"Hush! what noise is that?" inquired Minnie.

Minnie was being beaten at a game of chess, which had been begun the first night of Reginald's arrival, and which game was ever being disturbed by a certain housemaid, who could never be brought to understand what a vast difference the displacement of a single pawn makes. As Minnie once observed,

> "A pawn just on the crowning square,
>   A little pawn it was to her,
>   And it was nothing more."

The consequences of the deeds of this housemaid were grievous. Why are not housemaids taught chess?

"Hush! I hear something, I am sure," Minnie again cried.

They listened: the winter wind is not so musical as this. The small birds' voices have long ago been hushed, and yet it is the voice of many birds all singing in harmony. They are the fledglings Mrs. Neville took care of in the summer, repaying her now with songs of gratitude. His lordship and Aston were still closeted in the study, for gold wraps itself round men's hearts, and melts itself into men's ears, until they hear neither music nor poetry.

The songs of the children were echoing in Reginald's ears, as he went up to bed.

" Peace and goodwill to men; " what precious words are those sung by innocent children's lips ! " Peace and goodwill to men," said Mrs. Neville, as she wished him good-night. " Peace and goodwill to men," she said, when she first met him on the morrow.

The children had evidently made a great impression on her; their visit was so unexpected. And Reginald could see, when they were all gathered in the hall, the tears rolling down Mrs. Neville's cheeks. Were they of joy for the poor children's happy looks, or sorrow for her husband's apathy ? Who shall say ?

The next day Mrs. Neville drove to Stoke Furnace, and bought the poor children some clothing; but she did not tell her husband. The great game at chess was put aside for a longer period than usual, and Mrs. Neville and Minnie were busy making capes and cloaks for the children.

"We must not even overdo this," said Mrs. Neville, in answer to an observation of Minnie's upon almshouses. "Depend upon it that charity overdone is the most uncharitable thing in the world. Take Lord Grandpound's place at Grandpound, where he has built almshouses for old men and women, but where young men and young women would go if they could. It is very good of his lordship to build these hospitals for age, with a Latin inscription, *piæ senectutis domus*, which Alfred Craven translated as 'a pious old house.' But was there ever so much misery in a village as in Grandpound? Happiness is not attainable by the artificial means of almshouses. Walking with crutches is not pleasant for a man whose legs are sound."

Minnie was hardly convinced. She had plans of her own for setting the world's broken joints. A dreamer of pleasant dreams was she. Grandpound was a model village a few miles off, where most wonderful experiments, or rather tortures,

have been practised on the labourer by good-
meaning philanthropists, who have admirably suc-
ceeded in making him twice as discontented and
unhappy as before. But, as Mrs. Neville observed,
"we must not be discouraged by Lord Grandpound's failure; I should have been much surprised if his schemes had ever been successful."

Her speech was here stopped by Lord Cokeborough's appearance. His lordship was for
making railroads all over England, and thereby
improving the moral condition of the labourer.
Worse opinions than this have made some eminent
statesmen.

The weather became colder, but the raggedness
of the children had long been sewn up, and " The
pond will bear," is the news at breakfast this
morning.

"It is the only pond in the neighbourhood,
and we are sure to have a good many people here
to-day," observed Mrs. Neville.

" What, Minnie, you don't skate!" said Reginald.

" Indeed I do; but you must come and help

me, like a good cousin. We must go into a quiet corner of the pond; I cannot bear to start with a number of people looking at me."

The pond is some little way from the house, but they soon reach it. Already a good number of people have come, for a flag has been hoisted on the top of the hall as a signal. Minnie can skate very fairly, but she is a little timid at first. "Now please hold my hand fast;" "Now, are you quite sure the ice will bear?" and other little speeches like these are heard before Minnie is fairly launched. Lord Cokeborough has found the ice-chair, and is driving it fast and furious.

"Will you take a seat in my train, Miss Neville?" his lordship inquires; but Minnie prefers skating.

"Now, don't go away, Reginald, but stop with me."

Little Flo and her governess have just come. The governess, Miss Minson, has tied bands of list under her feet. Flo is only beginning to learn to skate, and it is some time before they get her shod, as Minnie termed it.

"Oh, Miss Minson, please stand before me, every one is looking."

This little speech is made whilst Flo is being shod, to repeat Minnie's expression,—a rather delicate operation.

The pond is not so large as the lake at Mere-pool, but it is prettily situated in the centre of deep woods, whilst great green scarlet-beaded holly-trees fringe its banks in all directions, and give it a picturesque look. The ice has frozen very smooth and very hard, as Lord Cokeborough can tell by that last tumble.

"Engine run off the rails, Lord Cokeborough?" Miss Minnie cries.

"Rails are rather slippery, and I want a new flange to my skates," says his lordship, talking in railway language. "Now will you take a seat in the excursion train?" he continues, catching hold of the chair again; but Minnie declines. "Here is Mrs. Beach; I know she will be a passenger." So Mrs. Beach is persuaded to enter the train.

Mrs. Neville now comes down at the head of

a large band of ladies, who one and all declare that if the others will go on they will. There is Miss Pinder, as light as a feather, is sure the ice will break with her, although it bears fat Mrs. Heavysides.

"My dear Miss Neville, I cannot think how you dare venture to skate," half-a-dozen ladies' voices exclaimed. But Miss Minnie only vouchsafes a gracious bow of the head and a smile, and the slightest little wave of her parasol, as much as to say, "See how easy it comes to me." The players at hockey all stop as she glides by them, skimming the ice as the swallow does the water, just marking her way with little tiny strokes.

"How ever did you learn?" asks the light Miss Pinder, who is sure the ice will not bear her, now that Minnie has come back to the spot where all the ladies are congregated.

"Used to practise on the polished oak floors all the summer," Miss Minnie replies, with a smile.

"Now, do show me how you do it."

This is quite impossible, as Minnie to-day wears a longer dress than usual to prevent any one seeing how she does it; and you can only catch a glimpse of the sparkle of her skates as she glides along like an automaton figure on wheels.

"Not had one tumble to-day, Reginald; I wish, though, you would help poor Flo."

Flo has not dared to come out of her snug corner, and she is practising behind a chair. Minnie joins her sister, and she and Reginald take Flo between them and skate with her all round the pond. Mrs. Beach, after having been nearly upset in her special train, has got out, and is vegetating in the middle of the pond like an ice-plant. Flo is becoming tired, and Minnie is seen once more by herself gliding about the throng. Her face sparkles with animation and expression; she knows she can beat nearly every one here, and is proud of it.

"That girl must have been brought up in Holland, and skated up the Dutch canals with the butter and eggs to market," cries the jealous Mr. Parrot.

You can tell where Parrot has been by the ruts in the ice. Alfred Craven and his friend Leighe have arrived. Alfred Craven skates very much like those insects which are seen sprawling and struggling about on the ponds in summer. It is very cruel of Miss Minnie to ask Mr. Leighe to bring her a biscuit, and Mr. Parrot to fetch her a glass of wine, for luncheon has been sent down from the hall. Mr. Parrot attempts to bring her the wine, but cruel Minnie has before this skated to the other end of the pond, and Parrot is slowly stumbling after her, whilst Mr. Leighe is circumambulating the pond like a French poodle that dare not jump into the water. When, at last, Miss Minnie does choose to come to the ill-used Mr. Parrot—for he could never have reached her—of course long ago all the wine has been spilt. Miss Minnie thinks she had better take the glass herself.

"You may tumble down with it, Mr. Parrot; and you know how dangerous a wound is from broken glass;" and away sails cruel Minnie.

There is a ball at Bushwood this evening; "and you must not tire yourself too much," says Mrs. Neville to her daughter; but Minnie is in much too high spirits to care for the future. She would have played hockey, if it could have been done with any propriety; and Reginald saw her give the cork an accidental tap with her parasol, as she glided in and out among the players. She would have carried it away from most of them in capital style.

Reginald's thoughts were turned upon old times at Merepool, and he could not help contrasting the present with the past. The old solitary lake with its tall reeds, and wild-fowl flying overhead, reappeared. The cold frozen echo, the long dark shadows of the trees, the wild cry of the snipe, he fancied he again heard them all. He stood and listened, but solitude and grief and silent indignation were now turned into deep joy and gratitude.

"You will be my partner to-night, Regy, for the first waltz," said Miss Minnie, somewhat blushing, to him at dinner.

"But I have," he replied, " as much idea of waltzing, as Mr. Parrot of skating."

"How very provoking! I had a notion you could do nearly everything; how is it waltzing is not one of your accomplishments ? "

He was obliged to confess that at Merepool dancing was not thought necessary for him, and in addition, that the Misses Ancaster would never have condescended to have danced with him; " and on that account I never discovered the misfortune of being unable to waltz."

" I must turn dancing mistress then," she replied; " for, however do you think," she continued, in a mocking manner, " you are to rise in this great world when you cannot dance?" and Reginald somewhat believed in Miss Minnie; and if some young gentlemen of his acquaintance would own the truth, they would tell you that they obtained partners for life by simply being able to waltz in a superior manner. There was young Mr. Post Horne, who danced himself into ten thousand a-year at the last Ironshire county ball. It is not, perhaps, a very good way of obtaining ten thousand a-year; but are there not many worse means commonly practised?

The ball-room at Bushwood was seldom used. Fires had been burning in it for several days, and chairs and sofas, like so many snakes, had suddenly cast off their brown-holland skins.

"Why did you not tell me this before, Regy?" said Miss Minnie; "we should have had time to have given you some practice in the schoolroom, with Flo and Miss Minson. I shall be teased all night with Lord Cokeborough."

"Is that your only reason for wishing I could dance?"

"You don't think so, do you, Regy? No, it is the pleasure I should have in dancing with you," she replied, knowing Reginald was only joking.

"It is very stupid of me, is it not? But we must have a longer walk to-morrow together, and I shall have the pleasure of learning dancing from you, so we shall both be gainers."

Night drew on, and Minnie came down dressed more beautifully, and looking, too, more lovely

than Reginald had ever seen her. It is useless
for me to describe her, for, as Congreve says, " it
is the lover that makes the beauty." Reginald
thought her perfection. He gave a sigh as he
remembered he should not be able to dance with
her.

" How pretty you look ! " said he; "do stand
still while I admire you," and Minnie's large eyes
beamed down upon her cousin like two of the
fairest stars that ever beamed on mortal's destiny.
And she, too, thought him perfection, with his
delicate, yet firm features, almost womanly in
their expression of tenderness and kindness, and
yet so manly.

" I am so vexed with my stupid self," he again
said; "come let us have a walk by ourselves up
the long passage," and the two cousins walked
up and down the long corridor, arm in arm, and
hand in hand, in the darkness. But they must
go, as the ball will soon be opened.

The band is playing. The whole room is in
motion; but poor Reginald is anchored on a crim-
son cushion. Feathers and head-dresses nod in

endless confusion. Minnie seems still to be skating, and gives him a kind smile as she flashes by on Lord Cokeborough's arm. The music has ceased, and she walks up and condoles with him on his desolate condition. Old Mr. Golding says:

"Don't you dance, Mr. Reginald? a young man like you and not dance? there's my daughter will be most happy to try the next polka with you." The rich Miss Golding is being besieged with partners, so that Miss Eglantine Beach, who is neither rich nor pretty, and, therefore not overburdened with partners, is ready to stab her. Alfred Craven looks down upon poor Reginald, as he passes with that flirt Miss Ogle on his arm, with an expression of quiet contempt.

"Not dance, Mr. Neville? I never heard of such a thing; come, you are lazy," says Mrs. Beach, who is looking for a partner for Eglantine. The band again plays. What would poor Reginald give to join the throng? Minnie is still skating, as it were, over the boards. Reginald can't take his eyes off her. This polka will last for ever, he thought, and every one inquiring of him, why he does not dance; till at last in self-defence, he turns upon his principal tormentor, Mrs. Beach, and hopes he may have the pleasure of the next galop with her. She never does such a thing as dance, but she will, she positively will. Minnie observes them, and is half angry he has not asked her instead.

" Why, Reginald, I thought you never danced!"

" No more I do," was the reply.

" You are joking, Mr. Neville," cries Mrs. Beach, in amazement.

" Indeed I am not ; I never galoped in my life."

" Eh ! what? I declare; and so you were going to have an experiment with me ; a very pretty tale." And the old lady thanked her stars for escaping an inevitable fall, which must have attended their performance. Reginald conveys Mrs. Beach back to her couch, and she falls into a most learned dissertation on various ladies' head-dresses. Every bud has as many faults as Mrs. Beach generally contrives to find in their natural state.

" The gardeners too,"—by the gardeners Mrs. Beach meant the milliners,—" arranged them so badly; " and then she went on to show what a useful thing it was when mortals could not have real, they could have artificial flowers.

Miss Ogle has left Alfred Craven for young Lord Bureau, a rising politician of republican principles, whose maiden speech in the House was so praised the other day in the *Dew*. Miss Ogle is saying how she admired it. Lord Bureau is supposed to have been in communication with the Chartists on the famous 10th of April.

" Such shocking principles! I can't understand them even. Now do tell me what the Charter is; and did you really mean to make Cuffy prime minister? I could have understood it, if they had placed you at the head of the Government."

Miss Ogle's flattery is of a very broad character, but this is not so disagreeable to Lord Bureau as to be perfectly insupportable. " And then you were to do away with all titles, and the clergy, and the taxes; how funny it would have been! " Lord Bureau glories in his republican principles. He has never spoken to his father, Lord Despatchbox, for the last three years; and is enthusiastic on this particular, perhaps more so than concerning the former. Everybody, wherever he goes, endeavours to turn peace-maker—people love to bring two estranged coronets together—but the young nobleman assures them it is impossible, and everybody goes into convulsions of grief at this sad business, all which convulsions make the young man more certain that a reconciliation cannot take place; and everybody cries out, " Oh, these sad, sad politics! poor dear Lady Despatchbox, what must she have suffered!" and whenever this is uttered, the young nobleman looks more heroic and defiant than ever.

Minnie has been dancing all night. She and the rich Miss Golding have been overdone with partners. She, however, contrives to get a rest for a few minutes, and comes and sits by Reginald.

" Look at your friend Mr. Leighe waltzing with Miss Ogle," he said.

" I see them; it is not often two ladies waltz

together;" and Miss Minnie amused herself with several similar satirical observations on one or two other partners; but they were all said in such a laughing good-natured way, that the sharpness of the sting was blunted.

"We will go up to poor Flo and Miss Minson in the schoolroom, if you like; they must be very dull, poor things," she continued; so they slipped out of the room.

But Flo and Miss Minson were not at all dull. They had had the cream of the supper sent up to them, and were enjoying themselves famously.

"Here is Reginald cannot waltz, cannot even go through a quadrille."

"You don't mean to say so, Reginald! Mamma brought word just now, that you were about to have a galop with Mrs. Beach," said Flo.

"Well, you can learn a quadrille in ten minutes with a good memory and a little assurance: what do you say, Miss Minson, to a ball up here? I am quite ready. Will you button my gloves and be my partner, Reginald?" said Minnie, all in smiles. Miss Minson was quite willing. She was a good-natured little woman, ready to oblige, anybody.

"I will be the gentleman, and whoever is disengaged must play the piano," she said.

So they begin. And Reginald suddenly found himself a dancing shuttlecock, now here, now there, never resting for a moment; now to the right, now to the left, and now down the centre. But by the time he had learnt the third figure, the two preceding, with all their beautiful variations, had long slipped his memory, and at the close he finds all the figures, with several more new ones, of his own invention, running in his head. Great praise, however, is awarded him, and it is confidently asserted that he can go through a quadrille, which he totally disbelieves.

"I will put you right, you know, if you will dance with me," said Miss Minnie; and Reginald makes a rash promise.

When they go down-stairs, a quadrille is being commenced. Some one is frantically looking for a *vis-à-vis*. They rush in, and fill the vacant spot,

21—2

and plunge into the mysteries.   Where he is, what he is doing, Reginald knows not. Miss Ogle is performing a war dance before him, evidently expecting that he shall assist her.   Minnie whispers he should give her his hand.   He gives it, and Miss Ogle leads him into the centre.

"Do I perform a war dance before her, or what?" thought he to himself.   Luckily there are other gentlemen also in the centre, and he imitates their movements; but since every gentleman has a unique movement of his own, this considerably puzzles him; but he keeps moving, which appears to be the secret of all dancing.

"You are excellent, Reginald, better than I expected," whispered Minnie.

Miss Ogle is one of those intrepid dancers, who always seem inclined to knock their *vis-à-vis* over, as if they were simply put there as soft buffers to run against.   But Reginald gallantly disputes every inch of ground with Miss Ogle. He looks a calm defiance at her, even as she looks at him, and they thus mutually learn to respect one another.

But the quadrille is over, and Reginald returns to his former non-dancing condition, for the next is a waltz. Another quadrille does not come till the very last; but there is *contre-danse* soon, which Minnie tells him is also entirely mechanical, and encourages him that he can perform, if they become the last couple. At present, therefore, Reginald goes back to his couch, which he finds is occupied by three elderly ladies. The first is Miss Speltzer, aunt to the rich Miss Golding, and who has been watching that young lady's movements all night with remarkable vigour, as she is always expecting some one to run away with her niece. She is nervous whenever her niece and her partner go near the door. She is ever thinking of carriages and four horses waiting for her niece in lonely lanes. Miss Speltzer wears curls, like long white deal shavings planed from her forehead, which appears smooth and shiny in consequence. The other is old Miss Tatler, who wears her dress very low with an edging of swan's-down, so that about the neck she has the appearance of an antiquated vulture. And the

third is the Dowager Lady Rickminster, who
wears on her head a turban like a grindstone,
that bows her down. Beside them is sitting the
Rev. Professor Ammer, the great geologist, who
has lately reconciled the Mosaic account of the
creation with the latest development theory, whose
forehead is bold, rugged, and stratified, as if his
brain was cropping out. He used to frequent
churchyards on purpose to see the graves dug,
and report states that once, instead of saying
" dust to dust, ashes to ashes," he gave out
" clay unto marl, and ashes unto oolite." It is
also said that he drained the whole of his vicarage
farm on purpose to dig out the fossils, and that
he was once caught hammering away at Lady
Purbeck's marble chimneypiece, by the housemaid, who not unnaturally thought the learned
professor had gone mad.

But the ball finishes, even as Reginald's first
quadrille. Morning is breaking, tired visitors are
going away with headaches, when they of course
pretend to be not the least fatigued.

" It has been such a delightful ball!" Miss

Eglantine Beach, who says this, is ready to swear at the ball.

A week after, a children's party is given for the benefit of little Flo, and Reginald is appointed steward on the occasion. There is exactly the same fluttering of head-dresses and nid-nodding of heads as before. Little Miss Beach wears the same wreath of violets as her sister did, scented just as they are in nature, only twice as much. Miss Ogle is there again in the shape of her little sister, and Reginald learns as much of human nature from the little Miss Ogle as from her elder sister; perhaps more. It is in smaller compass, and so more easily grasped. The little thing is flirting away with Master Pinder, a young gentleman given to low spirits, who, when Reginald asked him if he did not dance, replied, with a sigh,—

"Thank you, my dancing days are over," but somehow or other he presently contrived to waltz with Miss Ogle. Now there is the first quadrille, and Reginald with some difficulty marshals little Master Tom Tucker and little Miss

Pinafor with their *vis-à-vis*, Master Bib and Miss Tom Tucker, but at last he finds it is a great condescension on the part of Master Tom Tucker to dance a quadrille at all, which he "walks through," as he says, with much dignity.

"Which will you take, Miss Tom Tucker?" says Master Briggs; "a strawberry or lemon ice?"

"Thank you, Master Briggs, I never eat ices," says this precocious little lady; "I consider them very dangerous things, especially when you are dancing in a warm ball-room. Why do they not have the windows up?"

At this hint Master Briggs rushes off to open one of the big windows, which fortunately he is not tall enough to reach.

"I do think Miss Ogle is more odious this season than ever; did you ever see such a style of waltzing? She is positively hugging Lord Infants round the neck."

Young Lord Infants has never asked Miss Tom Tucker to dance with him, perhaps this has something to do with the remark. In the meantime,

Lord Infants and Miss Ogle have approached the refreshment table, and his little lordship gives it out as his firm opinion that strawberry ices are not near so good as they were some years ago, in which remark Miss Ogle coincides in theory, though she has eaten three already.

Ah, yes, this strange human nature is the same in degree in all of us. Look here, how this little Miss Ogle nods her head about in the same manner, and dances in the same style, and flirts, like her sister, with only a favoured few. This child is the mother of the woman. Look how the young gentlemen from public schools have a great contempt for those at private establishments; how young gentlemen in coats look down upon those only in jackets; and how the young gentlemen in jackets despise those only in frocks; and how the young gentlemen in frocks, but with pockets in their trousers, despise those who have frocks, but who have no pockets in their trousers; and finally, how these young gentlemen in frocks, but pocketless, and therefore penniless, have still a very good opinion of themselves; and I should like to know if this is not just the case in the real world of men and women?

The balls are not yet over at Bushwood; the servants are to have one, and they may invite other servants.

"We must wait upon ourselves to-night," says Mrs. Neville.

So they divided the various duties, and did not give themselves many more airs than most servants.

"Come, Mr. Reginald, decant the .wine, and don't be too long, or we shall really think you are the butler," said Minnie.

And Miss Minnie herself made a very pretty pert maid-of-all-work, and did not break many more things than that hard-used servant generally does.

"What do you say to going to the servants' hall and seeing how they get on?" asks Minnie.

Minnie would have gone and danced there in a minute. So some of them do go, and peep in

at the servants' hall just as the servants did at
the night of the ball. The servants had evidently
taken their cue from their masters and mistresses,
or had their masters and mistresses taken it from
them? One or the other, it does not matter
which, when both do it so to perfection. Rag-
gles, the Bushwood butler, is acting his master's
part beautifully. How he flatters those two spin-
ster upper housemaids, and the old dowager
housekeeper! The shade of Gil Blas wandered
here to-night. Lord Bureau would be jealous of
the republican principles of his valet, which the
latter is broaching to the kitchen maid. Could
Miss Ogle flirt more openly with Lord Plaid-
tartan than her lady's-maid does with his groom?
Could Mr. Parrot talk much more illiterately of
books than his man? But why should they not
all enjoy themselves as well as their betters?
We will not make sport of them. It is not often
their labour is sweetened with laughter. I for
one agree with Miss Minnie, though she first
proposed the expedition, that " it is a shame to
stand peeping and prying at them; how should

we like it?"   So they all come away, and are
right glad to hear the honest laughter ascend-
ing into the drawing-room, and to be told the
next day by the housekeeper that everybody enjoyed themselves.

CHAPTER III.

THE QUARREL AND RECONCILIATION.

THE frost still continued, and Minnie was as
fond as ever of skating. Flo, too, was improving, and no longer wanted the company of a
big kitchen chair. Good-natured Miss Minson
was also induced to put on a pair of skates; but
the little woman unfortunately received a serious
fall, which laid her up for a day or two.

"I know you can catch me, Reginald; but
you are the only person who can," Minnie used
to say; "but you go and join them at hockey,
or whatever it is called."

So Reginald would sometimes leave her and
play, and when once he had hold of the cork,
no one there could overtake him. And Minnie
used to watch him with delight, beating every-

body. Parrot used to station himself half way down the pond, waiting till Reginald came by, but he invariably fell when he made a stroke. It cost him at least two more tumbles, before he was again on his feet; so that there was some truth in Miss Minnie's pert saying, "Three falls make one get up, Mr. Parrot, don't they?" But she meant him no harm, and the next minute would be brushing the snow off his back with the end of her parasol. The frost could not freeze her good spirits.

In the evenings now, they were busy rehearsing charades, and small pieces in one act—for their company was small, and their scenery very limited. Minnie now turned from stitching poor children's clothes to making theatrical dresses. The ball-room was easily converted into a theatre.

"What shall we have for our drop-scene?" asked Minnie. "Last year we had a scene from the iron country, with all the furnaces and chimneys spouting terrific flames; what say you to the old pond, with a number of figures skating in costume? it will be far better than those wretched allegories we can buy."

So they converted an old lumber-room at the top of the house into a stage-carpenter's shop, and were soon busy painting with very big brushes.

"This comes of having had a French governess," said Mrs. Neville, as she entered the *sanctum.*

Mademoiselle Francisco, who appears first to have given her pupil a taste for theatricals, has been invited to stay a week this Christmas at Bushwood.   She is quick and sprightly; and seems to think she is ever on the stage.   She left Bushwood when Miss Minnie's education was completed, and went to live with a wealthy London silk mercer, whose family is brought up in Low Church principles, and a general abomination of the stage.   She is relating to them all the dismals of her present life; and, at the same time, suggesting how she should like to come back and teach Flo; and, to tell the truth, Miss Minnie would have no objection, for she is very fond of mademoiselle, who makes a most lively

companion, far better than quiet Miss Minson,
who is very good-natured, but a little common-
place. Mademoiselle would take any part or
character; work at anything, attempt any difficulty, as long as the stage was connected with the
matter; and since, as has been before said, the
stage was ever in her mind, there was nothing
in this world she would not undertake.

How they mismanaged their performances, it
is not necessary to relate. Sufficient it is to say
that the drop-scene, which was so universally
admired, did not always rise or fall with great
precision; that some of the actors had not very
good memories; and that the prompter's duties
were rather onerous. Miss Minnie, every one
allowed, acted uncommonly well. It is also quite
true, though, that this young lady, like other
great performers, sometimes chose for herself the
best parts; that she sometimes, too, sang a song
or made a joke, which was not in the piece; that
she used to dress for her part—if it was a pretty
dress she had to wear—considerably before the
time; that she used afterwards to forget to rub

off quite all the rouge from her cheeks; that she had a little quarrel with mademoiselle about some dress or other; but these are matters which should never be repeated, and are simply told here that the reader may see that Miss Minnie, with all her flow of high spirits and good-nature, was not quite beyond the reach of vanity.

"Who is it that writes to you, Regy, in this pretty hand?" exclaimed Minnie, one morning, when the letters were brought; "I should so much like to know who your correspondent is; now, do let me read it!" and Miss Minnie gives a little tug to pull it away, but Reginald held too firm. "So you are not going to read it now?" as Reginald put away a letter of Miss Garland's, which he did not wish to show. "Now do tell me the lady's first name; well, tell me only the first letter," and Minnie runs through a variety of names, and the alphabet several times over. "Well, then, give me the envelope, if you will not tell me her name, or the first letter, and I will decipher her character from the pretty handwriting: now there is no harm in that." So Reginald gave up the envelope. This was merely a trick of Miss Minnie's to catch a sight of the note. Of course she did not wish to decipher the handwriting, and simply tore the envelope in pieces, and flung them into the fire; adding, she should like to serve the letter the same. But she has taken good care to look at the post-mark: all this was done before the rest came down to breakfast. Miss Minnie's fine eyes were full of mischief during the whole of breakfast, and she talked most of the time in French to mademoiselle, and, as Reginald knew just enough of that language to confuse him, he took hold of precisely the wrong sense, as a deaf person misunderstands the drift of a conversation.

"You are coming up to the rehearsal of the new piece, I suppose?" said Minnie, as she left the room; "we shall be ready in about an hour's time." Reginald was rather late. "Why, we thought you did not intend to come," cried Minnie. Reginald laid the blame on the shoulders of time. "You have been so occupied with that letter, I suppose," was the only response.

But why has Miss Minnie taken such pains to dress herself for a mere rehearsal? She has dressed herself for her part in reality, though to-day she only half acts it. Formerly she used to act it in reality at rehearsals, and only dress for it at night. And when they come to a part where Reginald is bidding her adieu, about to perform certain impossibilities behind the scenes, she coldly touched his hand, and does not even bid him stop, that she may share death with him, and the direst tortures if they be needful.

So they remain for some days in a state of affection bordering upon politeness. Mrs. Neville notices something amiss, but Minnie laughs off her questions. It is the last night, positively the last night, of the Bushwood theatre. The new piece had been postponed, and there was another rehearsal of it to-day at eleven. Minnie always dresses now for rehearsal, and is looking this morning prettier than ever. They come to the

22—2

well-known passage, Reginald again feels a warm
hand enclosed in his.   He looks at Minnie's clear
eyes : he seems to read their meaning : he inclines
his head to the poor girl, and they kiss.   It is
a long silent kiss of forgiveness.   No one is
noticing them.   Those are real tears the poor girl
sheds.   She would willingly wipe out the past.
And those are not idle words she afterwards
speaks, that she would endure anything for his
sake.   Poor girl! she has rushed off to her own
room, for she cannot keep from sobbing.

She comes back to the drawing-room.   Reginald is standing in the bay-window watching the
thaw.   She comes to him, and begs pardon for
her unkindness.

"I really did not think I could have behaved
so, and am quite ashamed of myself," and the
poor girl burst into a flood of tears, and hid her
head against his breast, and then looked up im-
ploringly, with her eyes full of tears, into his face.
He could not help kissing her again and again,
as she clung round him still begging pardon.
"You are taking a bitter retaliation, Reginald,

by your silence; spare me now that I am thoroughly humiliated."

He could hardly speak, for he felt deeply, but at last assured her that he had quite forgotten the matter, and begged her to do the same.

"I know, Reginald, I have behaved shamefully; only say you will forgive me."

He in vain tried to show her he had no injury to forgive.

"No, I shall never be happy, until I hear you have forgiven me."

So he did, from the bottom of his heart. She raised her head, and he felt her warm lips pressing against his. He pushed back her hair, soaked with tears, from her forehead and face, and Minnie was once again her happy self.

"Here, Minnie, dear, you can read the letter," said Reginald, giving it to her.

"No, I do not care, Reginald; I will take your word."

"Yes, but whatever is mine is yours; but I did not think it at the time worth showing you."

"How. I wish I could help her! and was I so

foolish to be angry with you for this?" she said, when she read it, and Minnie felt that she loved Reginald twice as much as before, when she heard the story of the poor governess, and his kindness to her. That night the cousins sat side by side at dinner, and somehow Miss Minnie contrived to drop her fan or her glove oftener than usual, and she would try to pick it up the same time that Reginald did, and their two hands would meet with a long embrace. That night she played her part better, and looked handsomer than ever.

CHAPTER IV.

THE MEET AT MEDLEY GORSE.

THE frost was melting; the plates of ice were
thinner and thinner each morning, and you could
tell where the tide of winter had reached its
highest mark by the white surf-lines of snow.
Mademoiselle had gone back to the rich London
silk-mercer, and the theatrical wardrobe had been
packed up, for without mademoiselle they could
do nothing. She was stage-manager, prompter,
call-boy, scene-shifter, besides playing a couple
of characters in one act. Her "make-up" used
to be wonderful, and Miss Minnie sometimes
envied her skill in this particular, but Miss
Minnie was not far behind even in this; but being
far better-looking and having a handsomer figure,
was not obliged to have so much recourse to art
as her French rival.

The hounds met at Medley Gorse the next day,
for the first time after the frost. They were
generally known in the neighbourhood as Miss
Neville's pack, but Minnie disclaimed this. They
were not quite fast enough for her. Miss Minnie
has been teasing her father to raise his subscription this year, but Mr. Aston Neville will do
nothing of the sort. He merely subscribes, as it
is, that people may see his subscription. It is
not merely so much for the good of the kennels
as for himself. He cares very little about hunting; and his riding, like his politics, is of a very
safe character.

"Have you had much riding at Oxford, Reginald?" inquires Minnie.

"No, freshmen don't ride much," he replied;
but he and Amherst had been out once or twice
with the St. Matthew's drag, when Reginald
nearly staked one of Ippus's horses; but he
does not think it necessary to tell this.

. "You used to ride across country famously
with me in the summer," she continued.

Miss Minnie either had an objection to roads,

or else to paying turnpikes, and used whenever
she went out to take across country. "It is a
popular prejudice," she used to say, "that fences
are meant to keep animals within bounds; they
are simply human inventions of great ingenuity
for horses to jump; and I regard brooks as a
peculiar dispensation of nature, which break the
monotony of always leaping over hedges." Woe
to the unfortunate groom who had to follow
her, for mischievous Miss Minnie would choose
the hardest ground and the highest fences, not so
much to show off her own pluck and skill—though
partly, perhaps—so much as to perfect the groom
in his art. Reginald, as has been said, was never
allowed to ride at Merepool; but long before
the colonel and Lady Mary were down he used
to be out with the grooms exercising the horses,
and it was good rough practice, so that he had
not forgotten his riding. Who would have imagined one fine evening last summer when Minnie
so blandly proposed a gallop over Lindley Common, that she was going to ride ten miles over
hedge and ditch, as straight as the crow flies?

Miss Minnie gave the challenge with such a pretty bow of her head and such a smile beaming underneath her wideawake with the purple feather in it, that no one could have refused the offer. Reginald was only too glad of displaying his powers. Mr. Aston Neville had mounted him on one of his best horses, as he was afraid to ride it himself, and Reginald saw the groom grin as he vaulted into the saddle at the hall door, as much as to say, "You are in for a bucketing you are; I only hope you have a good seat, sir." Minnie's face sparkled as she galloped across the common.

"Over here," she said, pointing with her whip to a pleached hedge, and, gathering up her reins, was over it.

Reginald followed with Tearaway, making play as hard as he was able down a grass field, and nearly pulling off his arms. Minnie was now in her glory. Reginald looked up and saw the purple habit and the wideawake skating over the brook at the bottom, which Tearaway took in capital style. Minnie knew all the rolling grass lands for miles round, and they "bucketed" along, now by grassy deserted lanes, now by sheep-walks where the sheep fled before them.

"At last I have found some one who can ride!" exclaimed Minnie, when she pulled up. "You have not forgotten your riding, Regy, I can see: what fun we shall have in the hunting season together!"

And to the winter season Miss Minnie had been looking forward with vast pleasure; but the frost had stopped all hunting appointments till now.

"We shall have the horses sent on to the Crooked Billet, and you will ride your old friend Tearaway; and remember we shall breakfast early," were the last words Miss Minnie said, as she went up to bed.

The morning was dark and cloudy. But the black clouds rolled away; the winter sun slowly rose, and little fleecy cloudlets came driving before the wind.

"I am before you," said Minnie, reaching out one hand, and holding up her habit with the other, and pouting her mouth—for there is no one in the room but themselves—for an expected kiss. Mr. Aston Neville makes his appearance. Reginald rather envies his new scarlet coat with the buttons of the hunt, and those natty pink tops; but he somehow does not look cut out for work.

"I shall come and see the hounds throw off," said Mrs. Neville, as she entered the room with her habit on.

Lord Cokeborough, who is still staying at Bushwood, makes his appearance, but his lordship does not care for hunting.

"Why if you stray on the line, Aston, in your pink, the engine driver will mistake you for the danger signal."

The Right Honourable Robert Fynance, who is also there, of course does not hunt, but he will ride his old cob to the meet.

"Here, Reginald, put this in your pocket," said Mrs. Neville, giving him a pocket pistol; "I know you will want it before the day is over; and here are some hard biscuits."

"Do they still drink beer at breakfast at St. Matthew's?" asks Lord Cokeborough, who has been inquiring for "Bass."

"That is the sort of thing, Mrs. Neville," pointing to a silver tankard, "to pour it into."

Aston will not touch "Bass" at that time of the morning; but Reginald, who has already learnt the Elizabethan practice of drinking malt-liquors rather early, takes a good pull.

"Now promise me not to ride too hard to-day, Minnie darling," said Mrs. Neville; but she herself had been one of the hardest riders in the county, and Minnie had inherited her mother's disposition.

Miss Minnie has already finished her breakfast, and is pulling on her gauntlets and looking over to Reginald, as much as to say, "Be quick, finish your breakfast, and we shall have some fun presently."

Minnie has pulled off and on those little white gauntlets of hers, at least a dozen times. She has been to all the windows in the room and 'back again to her chair, and bent her whip double, and lashed it against her habit, quite tired of waiting.

"I wonder which is the worst country for hunting?" asked the Right Honourable Robert Fynance, musingly, as he took another egg.

"Why Breakneckshire, to be sure," replied Miss Minnie, rather pertly.

The great politician could not help laughing at Miss Minnie's bad joke. Just at this moment the horses came round. Little Flo's pony is there too. Flo has begged hard to ride to the meet, and she has come tripping down-stairs in great glee. Minnie would have liked Flo to have followed the hounds, but Mrs. Neville will not hear of such a thing. If the truth could be arrived at, that last tumble Flo had was occasioned by Minnie persuading her sister to leap Sheltie over a small ditch.

At last they make a start. Miss Minnie cannot wait while Lord Cokeborough is adjusting his stirrups as if they were the safety-valves of an engine. So she and Reginald ride on together to the Crooked Billet. Minnie is talking about her mare Diamond; "it was a very rough one when

I first had her, but you shall see how the dear thing carries me now." They ride along through bye lanes and cross lanes, for Minnie knows every short cut. At last they reached the Crooked Billet. It is nothing else but one of the small old-fashioned English farmhouses turned into an inn. Great oak beams in its walls cross and re-cross each other in all directions, forming a complete wooden alphabet, and a great wooden porch overhangs the doorway. The Bushwood groom is standing outside. Reginald lifts Minnie down. They can hear the hounds in the yard. Jim, the huntsman, makes his appearance with his old battered cap, the peak of which he seems trying to tear off in honour of Minnie.

"Very glad to see you, miss," he says, as he straddles out of the " Public " with his short legs. " You won't 'ave to complain of the 'ounds this season, miss; we have well weeded them, and drafted some in from the Bouchester pack." Jim is profusely civil to Miss Minnie, and makes sarcastic allusions to "tailors," as he calls bad riders, by advising them to follow Miss

Neville, if they can. It is more almost than Jim
can do himself, for Jim has seen his best days.
The whips are getting the dogs out of the yard.
Several stragglers are collecting round, and the
Bushwood party arrives, as the civil landlady is
bringing a chair for Minnie to mount Diamond.
But Minnie disdains a chair, and with her little
foot in Reginald's hand, and a slight spring, vaults
into the saddle, and is patting her dear Diamond's
neck.

" Now tuck my habit well in, Reginald; I
cannot bear to have it flying about me ;" and Miss
Minnie is at last seated to her satisfaction.

Reginald goes into the Crooked Billet to light
a weed.

" Law! sir, what a young lady that is, to be
sure," says the honest landlady; "howsomedever
she can do it, I can't a think: here, sir, here
is a lighter. Master Holloway, that is the huntsman, sir, was a saying that he had 'unted the
country for thirty years, but had never seen
the like of her afore. Bless your heart and
soul, sir, she'd think nothing of riding at a corn-

stack, or a corn-yard, for that matter; and yet sir, she is one of the most kind-heartedest creatures in the world."

Tearaway is now brought round, and the groom cautions Reginald.

"He hasn't had nothing to do, sir, 'cos of the frost." The groom's cautions are hardly needed, for Tearaway lashes out right and left, as soon as Reginald is across his back.

"How are you, Craven? but don't come near me unless you want a broken leg." Alfred is riding a horse almost as great a dandy as its master. A jolly old farmer comes trotting by with a peculiar hiccup, as though he were repeating "cuck-oo" at every step his jolting old horse took.

Reginald looks down as from a height, as he passes little Flo on her Sheltie. Mrs. Neville nods to him, and Tearaway takes it into his head to shy at her habit. There is rather a large field. The whips have got the hounds into the gorse; you can't tell their tails from their ears, as you see the black tips moving about.

Tearaway objects to his legs being pricked by the gorse, and will endeavour to put them into rabbit-holes, as a cure. This leads to an altercation between Reginald and Tearaway. It takes half an hour to settle the dispute, during which time the hounds have drawn the gorse in vain, and are now trying Medley plantations.

"Why, you are shirking work," cries Minnie, who has been acting as a sort of third whip.

"The fact is, I can't hold Tearaway in hand at all this morning, and expect to have some trouble with him."

"Now, Diamond, don't you be skittish too," and Miss Minnie rides off to the planting. Just then Wary gives a low growl, Watchful and Bounty and one or two more take it up; now the knell swells on the breeze. Suddenly a cry is heard of "stole away." Every one is standing in their stirrups, and they see a low red creature stealing along in a gallop down a hedge side, three or four fields off. The hounds are got out of the planting as quickly as possible. Minnie and clever little Diamond once more emerge.

"Gone away for Hambledon Hanger, for a thousand," cries a knowing-looking gentleman on a donkey.

"Will make for Topmoss Wood," cries a second on the same sort of steed. Everything is in bustle and confusion. The "tailors" are looking out for the gates and the gaps. Reginald has flung away the end of his weed, as a preparation for action, and his eyes glisten with excitement. The whole pack is streaming along a fallow.

"Now then, gentlemen, don't ride over the 'ounds," cries Jim, at the first fence which has just been cut, and which every one thinks himself bound to take.

"Don't try the fallow, Reginald, follow me," cries Minnie, as her mare takes a flight of rails into a grazing field. Tearaway follows, smashing the top-bar in his playfulness, and flinging the turf up behind him, like a patent plough. Away stream the hounds, but Reynard is three-quarters of a mile ahead by this time. The scent lies well. More timber, which Tearaway smashes as before: now the pace increases; it is killing off the

23—2

"tailors" very fast. Lord Cokeborough's horse, which he had sent on from Ironton on purpose, is puffing like an engine on one of his lordship's pet lines.

"This will do, miss, won't it?" says Jim, as he takes a hedge and ditch; "this pace will tail some of them off, I know." Tearaway thunders at the hedge, and leaps at least six feet over the ditch.

"Well held up, sir," cries Jim. But there is no time for talking. Right along Westaway Common they spin; down by Fludyer's brook, which is now swollen into a river. There is some one come to grief, but they have no time to stop. Past Tamerhill Church, and up the Hill Side. There are only six or seven in the first flight riding up to the hounds. Now at last there is a check.

"It's been a forty minutes' rattling burst; won't that do for you, miss?" cries Jim, in exultation. "Good dog, Beauty; now then, Trusty, hit it off."

In the meantime some of the nearest stragglers have come up. But they are all off again. All

those lingual bells are chiming. Tearaway begins
to enjoy the sport in grim earnest. On, still on,
along the ploughed fields, where the ploughman
stops his team to gaze at the mad race; down
past the village of Droynton, where the villagers
rush out of their houses to watch the wild storm
of horse flee by.. Still waves the wideawake
and the purple feather in the van of the hot
pursuit; still it leads the cavalry of the hunt—
still it proudly flaunts like a flag, over hedge and
ditch. No halt, no pause. The field is as thin
as it was before. The tall naked trees seem to
stare at the wild revelry, the leaves whirl, and
dance, and eddy on the pastures, as if they felt
the inspiration of the moment. And now there
is no one left but Jim, and the whips, and Minnie
and Reginald, and a stranger who rides with as
much boldness as good judgment; but he too
at last lags, then halts, and the rest feel as if a
limb had been chopped off from them. Who
goes next? There is a rasping hedge at the bottom
of the field. Minnie brushes it in fine style,
hardly shaking the scarlet hips from the thorns.

But the gray, with old Jim, swerves and refuses
it. Again he puts her at it, but she is dead
beat. Poor Jim! but the very hounds are tailing
off, and he can attend to them. On again: here
is Fludyer's brook once more. Diamond skims
it, and tucking her feet together, lands all safe.
Tearaway is as lucky. But the first whip is in.
There is no help, and they leave him nursing his
horse's head. And now only these two cousins
are left. Now they see Reynard again for the
first time. He is making for that dark wood
of firs in the distance—only a field ahead is he.
His spirits are drooping, and his tail is draggled
heavy with mud and wet. Still on: darkness
is fast falling. The wood is nearer than ever.
Tearaway begins to roll, but Reginald shoves him
through the next hedge. They are in the same
field with Reynard. The hounds see him. Now
there is silence, and now a long awful wail, as
they pluck up their spirits for a final spirt. One
more short field, and he is in the dark wood, and
safe for ever. They have no horn to cheer the
hounds, but Minnie waves her wideawake: there

is no need for that; save your strength for the last hedge. Now Wary, and Watchful, and Trusty are closing on him. The distance is becoming narrower—the hedge prevents them from seeing —now comes the struggle—they are running into him fast; only a few yards between them; and only a few yards between Reynard and the wood. Now 'tis reduced to feet—it is a race betwixt life and death—which has it?—Reynard is safe; he has leaped the ditch—no; he has fallen back—close upon the city of refuge is he slain. Poor fellow ! he deserved a better fate. There he lies gory and torn upon a bier of leaves—the six hounds that are up have hardly strength to worry such a noble enemy—they all lie side by side, the living with the dead—Diamond and Tearaway droop their heads, and Minnie and Reginald have a secret feeling with all their triumph of having won but a sorry victory.

Reginald takes Reynard up altogether—he cannot spare a hair of such a glorious fox—the hounds hardly grumble—there is a solemn stillness in the place—the sun is setting—he lingered to see the chase, and now is gone. The winter wind sighs mournfully in the bare flutes of the boughs, and against the sapless chords of the hedge. The runnel singeth solemn tunes: a pall of darkness is falling.

Which is the way? Where is the road? Not even Minnie knows. They have gone to-day even far beyond her track. They lead their poor tired horses, and the hounds slouch behind their heels. At last they find a gate, and after wandering some time make their way into a lane: in the distance a cottage light is shining, and they find they are at the village of Sleighton, at least thirty miles from Bushwood.

" This has been a glorious day," cries Minnie; " I don't mind being called the mistress of such hounds," patting one of their tanned heads. " You have carried me well, dear old Diamond," addressing her bay.

" But whatever shall we do, Regy, about reaching home ? " said she in alarm, when fully realizing their position; I fear poor mamma will be so frightened about us."

To attempt to reach Bushwood would be madness. There was nothing left but to seek shelter
at Sleighton. But with Reginald Minnie felt
herself safe, and he, as well as he could, quieted
her fears about Mrs. Neville.

At last they discover the principal hotel of the
village; it was but a tumbledown cottage, but
they were glad to find any resting-place.

"Lord a' mercy, master! do ye come here;
I never seed such a sight in all my life: whatever
is it?" were the first words the landlady of the
"Thatched Inn" uttered.

The landlord comes forth from the settle by
the fire, and philosophically contemplates the
strangers, with a long clay pipe in his mouth.

"Can we have something to eat, and beds
for the night?" asked Reginald.

"Lawks, now," says the master of the house,
in a contemplative manner, "I guess ye be the
Miss Neville of Bushwood, whom I have he-eared
so much talked on; ain't ye now?"

Minnie answers in the affirmative. The contemplative landlord regards her as he might

a goddess, in smoke and silence; till at last
Minnie breaks the spell by reminding him she is
hungry.

"Lawk now, I can assure ye I 'ae he-eared a
vast sight of talk about your riding," as though he
thought she was going to perform then and there.

"Come out, hounds!" this last is a remark of
Reginald's directed to Watchful and Wary and
some of their friends, who are thrusting their
noses into the kitchen. The landlady has come
back: she is far more energetic than her contemplative husband. She has been up to change
her apron; for though she asked, "whatever is
it?" as if Minnie was some unknown animal, her
quick eye had lighted on Minnie's gold chain
which hung round her neck. She wakes a
slumbering ploughman and ploughboy, and they
and Reginald extemporize loose boxes for Diamond and Tearaway, and shut the hounds up
in an outhouse. Minnie won't leave the stable
till she has seen her "dear Diamond" have a
warm mash, and they go back to the inn escorted
by the ploughman and ploughboy with their

lanterns, and the contemplative landlord's long pipe, which gives as much light as both lanterns. The bustling landlady has a fire lit in the best parlour, which smells sweet of lavender and apples. Some china mugs and plates with a considerable amount of reading in gold letters, as if, as Reginald observed, you were literally supposed to eat and drink " the feast of reason and the flow of soul," adorn the mantel-piece. Some slips of herb-honesty, with its dried, transparent, shining leaves; some wheat-ears of last year's harvest; a bunch of hops, also of last year's growth, ornament three vases on a side table, emblematic of the three constituents of English peasant life—Honesty, Bread, and Beer.

Minnie has gone up-stairs to take off the wide-awake and the skirt of her habit, and comes down smiling, the great flaring candle in its brass socket lighting up her sparkling features. The landlady now makes her appearance with a great dish of bacon, which foams with the white of eggs.

" Don't you enjoy this much better than a grand dinner at Bushwood, Regy? I know I do," cries Miss Minnie. "We shall want some more; I will ring," she continues, with a slight blush.

The bustling little landlady is in the room before the bell has done ringing; "she thought they would want some more, and so had it ready."

"And we want some more of your home-brewed beer," said Reginald.

She soon returned. The second dish vanishes faster than the first. Reginald this time rises, and with dignity pulls the bell.

"The woman will surely think we have been famished for a week," cried Minnie; "but I cannot help it; I am so dreadfully hungry."

"Would you bring another dish?" said Reginald, half apologetically; "and a little more beer at the same time."

Minnie hid her face; but as Minnie before said, "I can't help being hungry, the woman must think what she likes." The third dish arrived, the poached eggs looking like golden oysters on silver shells, as Minnie fancifully remarked.

They sat talking by themselves, wondering what would be thought at Bushwood of their absence, how well Diamond cleared this fence and those rails, how Tearaway took the brook, and so on. The fire burns brightly, and they could go on talking all night, but must be off to bed. Minnie will not go until she has been out to have another look at dear Diamond. Reginald had taken the stable-key, and they find their way. Tearaway and Diamond are both sound asleep. Diamond, though, hears her mistress's voice, and turns half round with a sort of " I see you " expression, and then again lays down her head. Tearaway snores on. Minnie comes back leaning on Reginald's arm. The winter moon was shining bright, and the cattle lay sleeping in the " crew " yard: a cock crows out from the barn, as if he were the village watchman tolling the hour. The watch-dog's chain glistens, and the yard pebbles gleam in the moonlight; the contemplative landlord stands smoking his pipe at the doorway, and salutes them, " Do ye now give us an account of the sport."

So they go into the kitchen, and Reginald turns
lecturer. The rustics from the bar come crowding in, and he soon has the whole village listening.
He received neither cheers nor groans, but plentiful " Ohs," " Lors," " Bless mes," " I nevers,"
" Lawks now," and with a supply of beer dis-
missed his audience. He gave Minnie a long
kiss on the staircase, and soon tumbled into
bed, and was hunting all night long in his dreams
on the back of Tearaway, with the habit, and
the wideawake, and the purple feather floating
alongside.

The morning sun was rising when Reginald went
down into the stables. Tearaway and Diamond
both looked tired. Minnie soon followed him;
and after breakfast the landlady sewed the skirts
to her habit again, and they left the " Thatched
Inn " with a group of idlers staring at them, and
the philosophic landlord smoking his long pipe
in the doorway.

" What a pity some good-natured fox would
not give us a run to Bushwood ! " cried Minnie,
as they slowly rode down the village street ; and

Miss Minnie would have been really delighted
in finding such a benevolent creature.   But they
were obliged to ride slowly, for it was evident
that Diamond and Tearaway were not up to
much to-day.   It was not till the afternoon they
reached the "Crooked Billet," where they left
their companions, the hounds.   Every one there
was wild to catch a single word about the finish.
Jim, it was reported, had said, "he could not
leave the hounds in better hands than Miss
Neville's."

"Bless my heart, miss, I never expected to
hear of your coming home alive.   Lord! you
must have flown like a bird, according to all
accounts," the landlady remarks; "they have
sent over from Bushwood this morning to inquire
if we knew anything about you; and I was afraid
what might have befallen you."

So they rode on and reached Bushwood just
in time for dinner.   Mrs. Neville had been not
a little anxious about them, and was growing
alarmed at their non-appearance.   She looked a
little grave when she saw them; "Well, mamma,

we really could not help it," and Minnie ran on
with an account of the position in which they
found themselves at the finish; "such a run will
never, perhaps, happen again in a lifetime," and
Mrs. Neville could hardly help smiling at Minnie's
description of the landlord and landlady of the
Thatched Inn.   Mr. Aston Neville had luckily
been obliged to go to London by the afternoon
train with Lord Cokeborough, and he did not
know of their absence, or Reginald's career
would have been cut short at Bushwood.   Already had he had a narrow escape.   Mr. Aston
Neville had closely watched him the night of
the ball, and not seeing him dance with Minnie,
but constantly engaged in a learned conversation, first with Mrs. Beach, and then with Professor Ammer, concluded there was nothing to be
feared.   Little did Reginald know how far his
inability to dance had been his safety.

CHAPTER V.

THE SEARCH.

Miss GARLAND still wrote to Reginald, looking forward to a change of circumstances, with that strong trust in Providence which inspires the faithful, so that they see the light of hope close to them, when to others there is nothing but a dawn of darkness. It was impossible, therefore, for him to glean anything very satisfactory as to her prospects. He fervently wished that Mrs. Neville would be able to obtain her some appointment, and he did not fail to remind her frequently of her promise. Lady Mary still resolutely refused to give Miss Garland a character. She would not compromise herself to society, as she said.

"Here is good news for you at last, Regy,"

said Mrs. Neville, one morning; "I have heard of a situation for Miss Garland; read this letter," handing it down the breakfast-table to him; "I think it will suit admirably; you must write to her immediately."

The situation was to take charge of a little girl whose parents were in India, but who was living under the care of an aunt in Oxenshire. So by the next post he wrote to Miss Garland, and Mrs. Neville also sent a short note, for she had quite interested herself in the matter.

"Why, this can never be an answer to mine so soon?" exclaimed Reginald, the next evening, taking up a letter from Miss Garland, which had just arrived. He tore it open — he was amazed when he read as follows :—

"MY DEAR MR. NEVILLE,—

"I feel I am acting wrongly in living upon your kindness. I have often told you so; but lately have felt the truth more and more. Forgive me for my present conduct, which may appear ungrateful, but my conscience dictates these lines. I owe you much, very much, which I can never repay. I am about to try the world unaided and unassisted, so fare you well; that you may prosper, will be the constant wish of yours ever sincerely,

"CAROLINE GARLAND."

And .then in a postscript were written these lines :—

"Fare you well ;
Hereafter, in a better world than this,
I shall desire more love and knowledge of you."

Reginald was thunderstruck. It was evident she had not received his note, and there was still hope. He would wait another post or so. In the meanwhile he vainly puzzled over the mystery. The reader may remember that when Reginald last saw Miss Garland, he fancied she said, "that it would be the last time they should ever meet;" but he had no opportunity to ask for an explanation. This now flashed upon him in a new light. He was at a loss, too, to comprehend the meaning of, "I am about to try the world unaided and unassisted." What could a frail woman do in this world? Women

24—2

in England have no profession to embrace; law,
physic, and divinity, are all of the masculine
gender, he thought to himself. To-morrow's post
came, but no answer. He determined to go at
once to London. Term commenced in a few
days, and he had a valid excuse for leaving
Bushwood. At Islington he learnt that Miss
Garland had left her lodgings, and did not intend to return. Mrs: Neville's note and his own
lay on the mantel-piece unopened. The landlady thought some one might call for them.
Everything of Miss Garland's was gone.

" Miss Garland was always very reserved with
me, sir; and I have not the slightest idea where
she is. She paid every farthing of her account;
I liked her very much indeed, sir. She was
very good and kind to my children; would take
them out for a walk, and give them lessons in
an evening, when she was at home; but lately
she has not been at home much." Reginald sat
musing. "You see, sir, she was a little given
to melancholy at times, and I have been afraid
that she might do something to herself."

Reginald looked again at her letter; those lines,

"Fare you well;
Hereafter, in a better world than this,
I shall desire more love and knowledge of you,"—

read to him now very differently than before. In despair he rushed off to the Bow-street station. He read in fear and trembling that death-list posted on the door, which the most careless passer-by must regard with awe. 'Tis a terrible return, worse than the list of killed and wounded in the bloodiest battle ever fought. For the dead here have all been at grips with a thousand spiritual enemies, which the soldier on the battle-field knows not. Reginald paused at the following words — " Female ; name unknown ; age, about twenty-six; black hair; dark eyes. Regular, well-formed, and handsome features." The policeman took him to the body-house.

" When was she found? " he inquired.

" Yesterday morning. She seems to have known better days; but we have so many of that class, poor things. They fling themselves off the bridges in a sort of madness."

They reached the charnel-house of the Thames.
The officer turned the key : he pointed to a
corner. Reginald rushed up to it. The face
was staring blankly at the ceiling, the black
hair hung clotted with mud over her brows ;
muddy stains were on her cheeks, and mud upon
her lips.

" Thank Heaven, it is not her," he exclaimed.

Another body lay there, a mere girl of four-
teen or fifteen. A small white bonnet with a
feather in it covered the hinder portion of her
head, revealing her poor sensual features ; a small
weak nose, a smaller and weaker chin, a large
mouth, whose teeth were enamelled, and cheeks
from which the rouge and pearl-powder were
not washed off, but had run together in hideous
mockery of health, whilst from her head had
fallen a braid of false hair. She, too, had sought
relief in the Thames, that Lethe of the moderns.
Reginald had no time to linger over the spectacle. He made his way back again to Miss
Garland's old lodgings, hoping still to elicit something from the landlady, but nothing was to be

learnt. Where could she be? begging and starving, perhaps, in the streets of London. So he hurried off to the office of *The Times*. There are three columns in that paper; I know not which is the saddest, that of deaths, or bankrupts, or the one in which Reginald begged Miss Garland to write to him.

He left the office not knowing what to do, and was first awakened by the sight of the Thames. The lights were lit on Blackfriars Bridge, and he watched the dark barges, like black creeping shadows, float underneath with the tide. He could not turn away. Here was the spot where that poor girl had sought relief for her woes early this morning. Who else may seek this medicine before another sunrise? some other sister of her wretched family. Kindly, O Thames! dost thou receive them into thy bosom! When the sea and the rivers shall give up their dead, the most wretched and most miserable will be thine.

Reginald lingered and loitered so long against the parapet, that he was afraid of exciting sus-

picion.   He hurried down Farringdon‑street,
and found himself carried with the stream along
Fleet‑street.   On he went past the newspaper
offices, underneath Temple Bar, along the Strand,
and by those biped lamp‑posts not half so pure
as their iron brethren.   He called at the old
place in South‑street; but the people there could
give no information.   It was now late; he turned
into bed at some hotel, but could get no rest.
He dreamt that he saw Miss Garland standing
on the bridge springing towards the water.   He
made a catch at her; but her clothes gave way,
and she fell shrieking against the parapet.   He
saw her standing with the wretched band of
claimants at the poor‑house, shivering in the
snow and frost, whilst the cosy overseer, after
dinner, snores by his fireside.   He saw her as
a basket‑girl with wreaths of flowers and nose‑
gays; but every one turned aside, and would
not buy.   He saw her with a troop of girls in
the finery of vice, over whom an aged beldame
watched.   He saw her lying dead in all that
finery.

The next morning he set off to all the police stations, and in vain made further inquiries: he had done all he could. The advertisement in *The Times* was to be repeated every other day for a considerable time. There was one more course—to employ a detective. Reginald did not hesitate. His instructions were merely to keep the matter quiet. The man noted down all the particulars, and promised to let Reginald hear soon.

CHAPTER VI.

COLLEGE LIFE.

THE days of a freshman depend so entirely on himself, that it is hard to fix any limit to them. The probation of one term finishes them for some, whilst others remain so all their time. After they have taken their degree, they are still freshmen; go into the world so; live in their country parsonages such; die so. Many freshmen of threescore and ten are there in this big world. But Reginald and his friend Amherst were fast emancipating themselves from their "green salad days." They were this term playing the part of host as well as guest, and in their rooms might be found men of almost every "set" in college: for St. Matthew's was in those days much split up into "sets." There were the hunting—including

the tuft-hunting—the boating, the dressing, the
reading, the billiard, and, worst of all, the do-
nothing "sets." And is it not exactly the same
in the world? Little De Ivery, when he goes
into the world, will simply graduate from one
fashionable dressing "set" into another. He will
but change "the High" of Oxford for Pall Mall.
He will but buy his jewellery and dressing-cases
from another goldsmith. The Marquis of Stirrups
will only emigrate from one hunting "set," into
another, from one saddle into another just like
it. But what becomes of the boating "set?"
Aye, what become of the "strokes" and the
"bows?" Whenever I see a skiff pulled down
some of our midland rivers, with that indefinable
style which belongs to Alma Mater, I say to myself, Perhaps here upon this unknown, unfre-
quented stream, is pulling some famous University
stroke. Poor fellow! he was once great in his
day, but must now be content to pull his wherry
on any ditch. As he sculls along, perhaps he
is thinking of the cheers on the banks of the Isis,
of all those tankards he won, which on high days

and holidays now grace his rectorial sideboard. One sad case was there of an old St. Matthew's man, poor Rollock, captain of the eight, before Reginald's day. He it was who brought St. Matthew's up to the head of the river. A great tall man he was, six feet two, with an affection for the boat, as for a human creature. On an unfortunate day, poor Rollock accepted a curacy in some part of England, where rowing water was not. Nothing but fields, fields ploughed, and fields grassy. At times he used to come up, and see how the old boat was going on, but it was remarked every time he was more thin and haggard. He tried in vain to have his curacy changed to where a stream ran. At last poor Rollock came no more to see his favourite boat. He died broken-hearted at his streamless curacy. And now a younger brother of his has come to St. Matthew's. Men who knew old Rollock say the young one is just like him, speaks like him, puts on his old ways, and reminds them of the poor old fellow. Young Rollock, though he came up the same term as Reginald and Amherst, was already stroke of the *Torpid,* and a general favourite with the boating men. They go regularly every day, even in this cold February weather, to practise. The old men come down to see their style of pulling. Lascelles, captain of the " eight," would run on the bank, watch in hand, to time them from the " Willows " to the " Long Bridges," and from the " Long Bridges " to Iffley. In the snow and the rain might the St. Matthew's *Torpid* be seen with its glittering blue oars, moving with a pulse-like motion down the river.

" I tell you what," said Lascelles, after they had " bucketed " down one day to Iffley, at least three minutes quicker than the day before, " I must have some of you drafted into the ' eight ' at once; there will be two men wanted, and I had better have you at once." So Rollock and Reginald for the future rowed in the " eight."

A glorious team that was, with little Bonnet, smallest of coxswains, sitting light as a feather, and turning the boat as though she went upon a pivot.

" We will have St. Matthew's head of the
' eights,' as well as of the *Torpid*," was the
theme of every wine party.

Even the dressing " set " began to take an
interest in the matter; and about three or four
o'clock on a March afternoon might be seen a
party of exquisites standing on the bank watching the St. Matthew's eight with every strength
of eye-glass. And by-and-by a report went
through the University itself that the St. Matthew's
boat would be head of the river.

" They have done the mile three seconds faster
than the Mark's boat," it was reported, and the
betting was on St. Matthew's; and the next day a
report spread that number five of the Matthew's
boat had sprained his left arm, and the betting
instantly changed. All this occurred some two
months before the actual race. And now the St.
Mark's men—for St. Mark's was head of the river—
began training in real earnest. And as the bright
weather came on, dinkies and skiffs, and punts,
that had all been laid by in hospital during the
winter, studded the water. The St. Matthew's

"eight" could no longer dash away from its moorings near the raft, as in the cold February days, for the dinkies and punts seemed only just convalescent after the winter, and moved but slowly out of the way, especially when manned by freshmen.

"Ship oars, bow-side: a narrow escape that," cried little Bonnet, looking daggers, and speaking them too, to some misguided individual who came across the path of the St. Matthew's eight, just as it was starting. So day after day did they "grind" down the river, and the whole talk of the University was the approaching race between St. Matthew's and St. Mark's, next term.

But we must retrograde a little. Of Miss Garland Reginald had heard nothing. The detective could discover nothing. From Bushwood he was constantly hearing. Amherst and himself became greater friends than ever. They breakfasted and read, and occasionally hunted together. There was a strong hunting set at St. Matthew's in those days. Young Snaffle, who won all the University drags, was a St. Matthew's man, and the Marquis of Stirrups kept a large stud at Ippus's, and gave his St. Matthew's friends a capital mount. Reginald could not afford to hunt often, or, in fact, at all; but the temptation, when there was a meet on a saint's day, was too strong to withstand. So the term soon ran its appointed length. Reginald and Amherst had done a good deal of reading, for next term they had to go in for "Smalls," or "Little Go," or "Responsions," as Pogis called it. "Collections" again came, and no more notice was taken of the freshmen than before.

"Alma Mater," said Amherst, "is exactly the reverse of a true mother, who takes care of her children when young, and leaves them to shift for themselves when older. Alma Mater only takes care of her old children, and that perhaps not in the best way."

Duns might be seen prowling about the "quad" the last week with their "little account," as a dun always calls his bill, no matter how heavy; and the Dons too made out their little accounts. Owen was noticed; in fact, expelled.

"Yes, if you wish to be noticed," said Reginald, "knock in every night after twelve ; but behave decently, and you shall be rewarded by hearing Slowcombe spoil Euripides, and Pogis confuse the Thirty-nine Articles."

Amherst very much wished Reginald to come home with him for the Easter vacation.

"We will read eight hours a-day, and take a 'pair oar' with us, for the river runs close to our house, and you will be able to keep up your reading and training as well."

But Reginald's love for Minnie prevailed over even his boating.

CHAPTER VII.

THE QUEEN OF THE MAY.

"Now, Reginald, I have had a study fitted up for you," said Mrs. Neville, as they drove back from the station; "and you can work there as much as you please without being disturbed."

"And I shall come and help you," cried Minnie, who was riding beside the carriage on her favourite Diamond.

"No; nothing of that sort if you please, Minnie," replied Mrs. Neville; "Reginald must really work hard, and gain himself a good position at Oxford, and then we will see what can be done for him."

So Reginald had a study to himself, and worked some six hours pretty closely every day. Sometimes, it is true, Miss Minnie would come asking him to go out with her and little Flo for a ramble in the woods. Fine early spring mornings were those, for Easter was very late this year, and Reginald used to sit reading with the window wide open, and the fresh spring morning breeze breathed in its sweet perfume, as he read the old Greek poets with a delight he had never before felt. Their verses seemed as fresh as the morning itself, as if but written yesterday, and not a thousand years ago.

"Stay a minute, Minnie, and listen to this," and Reginald would translate to her that most beautiful of choruses in the *Œdipus Coloneus*, or some of the exquisite *Idyls* of Theocritus, until little Flo, tired of waiting, would steal up to know what delayed them.

"You must let me hear this again," Minnie said, and she would often make this an excuse to come up, and Reginald used to translate to her all his favourite passages. Not content with this, Miss Minnie would make him turn them for her into English verse.

"But they are untranslateable, Minnie; as well

attempt to make humming-birds sing in our wild English woods."

"Well, come, we must go; here is poor Flo waiting for us; are you not, dear?" and she gave her little sister a kiss, and they hurried down-stairs and were soon in the thick woods.

Deep, thick woods they were, too, with rides cut here and there for shooting and hunting; but the cousins despised these aids, and were soon in the thickest parts.

"We shall have the keepers after us for disturbing the game," said Reginald.

But Minnie heeded not; on she went into the midst. The jays and the magpies screamed and chattered. The rabbits fled before them. The wild hawk wheeled above their heads. Little Flo could scarcely climb over the long trailing brambles, and Reginald stopped to help her, whilst Miss Minnie was far on calling them to come. Round their trunks the oak-trees were garlanded with the greenest moss. The ground was covered with golden tufts and clumps of primroses so thick that you might gather handfuls at a time, whilst here and there might be seen rising above them the taller ox-lips, and the still taller cowslips, straying away from the fields.

"Is this not fairy-land, Reginald?" said Minnie. "How pleased I am I did not accept Lady Bonnibel's invitation to town."

So on they went, treading upon thousands of primroses and violets, their feet quite muffled up in them.

"Oh, what a pity it is papa won't allow the poor of Stoke Furnace to come here!" cried Minnie: "such a sight as this would make them forget their poverty. Mamma has asked him a thousand times, but he won't."

Still deeper into the woods they plunged. The may was just opening its pure white blossoms; the larch was tipped with little fiery plumelets; the crab-tree was full blown; and deep in the brake they heard the newly arrived nightingale. On they went. And now, instead of primroses and ox-lips, they have suddenly come upon an azure wilderness of blue-bells, looking as if a strip of the dark blue sky itself had fallen piecemeal upon the earth. They can hardly tell them from the stream that flows and winds in and out amongst them.

" Who will race me to the hermitage?" cries Miss Minnie.

It is hardly any good trying, for Miss Minnie knows every path in the wood; she is already up the bank, and they can hear her merry laugh as she enters the old ruin. And now at last Reginald and little Flo reach it.

" This was no hermitage," said Miss Minnie; " a bitter sarcasm on the world to call it a hermitage; a hermit with all these flowers and trees, and birds, impossible! Well, it shall be no hermitage now; come, Flo, you shall be Queen of the May."

But little Flo could not be persuaded.

" Well, then, I will be," said Miss Minnie, taking off her straw hat. " To-morrow, though, is the first of May; but we shall be busy, so we will keep it now," and she shook out her long hair, and then folded it up loosely that the flowers might stay in it.

The difficulty was in the choice of flowers; they had enough to make a thousand garlands without stepping two yards. Reginald employed himself in weaving a simple wreath of white may, mixed with blue-bells and violets.

"Now, Minnie, let me put it on you."

"Oh, you stupid darling! the blue-bells are wringing wet, and the may is pricking my ear. I see you will never make a lady's-maid; I must put it on myself," and she ran off to the mirror of the stream, and came back smiling and beautiful. "There, how do you like me in it?"

Reginald gave her a kiss by way of answer.

"Well, then, I will wear it," said Miss Minnie, putting on her straw hat, for it was now time to leave.

At last they again emerged from the wood.

"There is mamma," said Flo, "coming down from the house."

"Why, you naughty children, where have you been?" cried Mrs. Neville. "I am afraid, Reginald, that Minnie is a sad truant."

Miss Minnie's face was hot and flushed with

rambling in the wood; her bright eyes sparkled, and her beauty was additionally set off by the crown of flowers. Mrs. Neville noticed it.

"I can see what you have been about. I am going down to the school to give the poor children a half-holiday to go into the wood, and pick flowers for to-morrow. As papa is away, I am going to take the responsibility on myself. So we will call at the gamekeeper's, and tell him to go with them; or else, if there are no pheasants this year, my poor children will be blamed."

Great improvements had been made at the school; and Mrs. Neville had now some thirty children. Poor little things! they stared at Minnie as if she were some goddess. Minnie took a class and heard their lessons, but they were all the time admiring her handsome face. The walls of the school were now papered with charts and maps.

"We have to thank good dear Mr. Golding for much of this," said Mrs. Neville to Reginald; "he actually sent me a cheque for a hundred pounds, and promised me a yearly subscription of fifty, he was so much pleased with the scheme ; so you see we can afford to keep a schoolmistress." The little things sent up their joyous huzzahs at the double intelligence of a whole holiday to-morrow and an invitation to the hall. In the midst of the excitement Mr. Golding and his daughter arrived. They had driven over to Bushwood, and walked down to the school-house.

" Do take off that wreath of flowers," said Mrs. Neville to her daughter, as Mr. Golding entered; but Minnie never dreamt of doing such a thing.

" Why, Minnie, you are Flora herself come again upon the earth," he said. Minnie take off that crown of flowers! not she. She wore it at luncheon, and at dinner too, that day ; and Reginald quite agreed with old Mr. Golding when he said, for the twentieth time :

" 'Pon my honour, Minnie, I never saw you look half so well."

Ever was Minnie the same bright, animated girl ; not like one of those streams, which in winter overflow their banks, and in summer are nothing but dry barren watercourses; but she ever possessed the same good spirits.

"To-day is the first of May," thought Reginald as he lay reading in bed next morning. Very early it was, and the first beams of the sun were just peeping in through his window and falling slantwise on the famous seventh *Idyl* of Theocritus, which he was reading. And in those words, "the first of May," what an amount of joy is contained! The first of May! the very words seem to smell sweetly; they look unlike all other words that ever were written. A magic spell is in them. The open "sesame" are they to the world of sleeping buds and flowers. Unbarred, unlocked instantly is all fairyland at their sound. The March winds have howled themselves away. April showers have wept themselves into buds. Blue skies hang overhead. The birds are singing; the birds, that chorus to the play of life, are chanting the old earth-song. So Reginald lay in bed musing and thinking, when suddenly he heard the sound of singing. It was Mrs. Neville's poor children singing in this new May

morning. They had erected a maypole on the
lawn, and were dancing round it. Little happy,
careless things! No potentate in Europe is half
as happy as yon little Queen of the May. No
millionnaire half enjoys himself as yon little boy,
her partner.

"Come, get up, Regy," cried Minnie's gentle
voice at his door,

'May will have no sluggardie abed,'

you know." And Reginald was soon down.

"Come along into breakfast, all of you," cried
Mrs. Neville to the children; and in they came
trooping, crowned with garlands, and holding
posies and nosegays in their little hands. Long
tables had been set in the hall for them. Piles
of bread and butter speedily disappeared. Minnie
was head-waitress; but even her activity could
scarcely supply the children's wants.

"What a capital waiter Briareus would have
made just now!" she said, as she put down two
more large dishfuls of bread and butter. "Come,
you are doing nothing, Regy."

"There is such a pleasure in seeing other

people happy, that I cannot forego the opportunity
of enjoying it," he answered, rather musingly.

Breakfast over, and the little things amused
themselves with sports till dinner-time. Dinner
over, and they played on till tea-time. Tea over,
and evening drawing on, the hall was cleared,
and blindman's buff and its like was the order
of the night.

Minnie and Reginald used to wander frequently
by themselves in those deep woods. Bright happy
days were they; only a few hours they seemed,
so quick they went. Often did those two find
their way to the hermitage, and on Reginald's
last day at Bushwood for the Easter vacation they
lingered at the old spot later than usual. Every
moment Reginald felt those warm fingers of
Minnie's more tightly entwined in his, and her
flushed face pressed closer. He confessed to her
his fears about her father's consent. But love
is ever silent. Minnie knew as well as he did
that it was an insuperable bar, but answered not
a word, only a long, silent kiss, the meaning of
which he could interpret, and warm, wet tears

ran down her face.   And yet they went away
happier from the old hermitage than ever they
had before been.   The stars, as they came out
from the wood, were shining brightly, like lights
in the dark blue window of God's house, and
seemed to glance kindly down upon them as they
went homeward.

CHAPTER VIII.

PLOUGH OF ST. MARK'S.

ALL Oxford was filling fast, for the gayest and the
brightest time was at hand. The " Little Go " list
was out and posted on all the buttery doors.
There Reginald saw his own name figuring close to
Amherst's, as " Reginaldus Neville-Aston e Coll.
St. Matt. ; " for now for the first time in his life had
he found the use of his second christian name.
The boating men were in great anxiety about
the two. Young Rollock had " scratched," for he
would have been examined somewhere just about
the races, as Reginald would have been, had he gone
in his proper turn. Never were there such inde-
fatigable "coaches" as the boating men. Lascelles,
the captain, and little Bonnet, the coxswain, worked
Amherst and Reginald in their four Greek plays

and Logic. And now the eve of the examination had arrived, and gentlemen whose names began with " A " trembled, for it was whispered that Plough of St. Mark's had determined to raise the standard of the schools. Morning came, and gentlemen whose names possessed the initial " A " might be seen walking, in white chokers, and faces as white as their chokers, in the school's quad. All the boating men had escorted Reginald and Amherst, as so many backers in the fight. "Little Go!" some of our readers will contemptuously exclaim; " what is Little Go to make a man nervous?" We are not all Cæsars and Hectors like you, my good reader. The clerk of the schools was there looking as if he would burst out into " *testamurs*," and " plucks." The doors are opened, and the victims go into the body of the room. The boating men and the public rush into a sort of gallery. Do you see that pale delicate lady standing far back and retired at the far end of that gallery? Poor thing! she is the wife of that gentleman commoner of St. Egbert's Hall, who is so nervously turning over his paper. He has been plucked twice before. Every time his pen stops, it sends a pang through her heart. And yet, though he has been plucked so often, she thinks him so clever, and is sure there is some mistake why he did not pass. Last time she waited for at least a fortnight in full expectation that her husband's *testamur* would be sent to him by post, firmly believing that somebody else had received it: and she is here again, full of anxiety and hope. A big stout man is her husband, whose name is Abbot, past forty, with full-grown whiskers, being examined by that beardless stripling, Plough. It is a humiliating scene to see this imp Plough torment the giant. Plough has no mercy. He has long ago discovered Abbot's weak points, and is rubbing the sore still sorer. One o'clock, and Reginald and Amherst have finished their papers, and are let out for luncheon.

"Floored your papers, Neville?" cried Lascelles, as a party of the St. Matthew's eight meet them at the school doors. "If Plough examines you as he did Abbot, I will fetch the Proctor," he continued; and Plough is freely anathematized by the boating men of St. Matthew's. Away they go to luncheon.

"Come, one glass more, it will steady your nerves;" and back they go to the schools, flushed and excited. Plough is looking over Reginald's papers.

"Neville-Aston, of St. Matthew's," cries Plough, in a sort of chilling curdling voice. Lascelles is as good as his word. At this moment, an irruption of more boating men takes place, jumping from one bench to another with much noise of boots, which makes Plough look surlier and fiercer than usual.

"The *Choæphoræ* of Æschylus you take up, Mr. Neville-Aston," said Plough, with a look as much as to say, "I have caught you now." Plough knows Æschylus by heart, and does not condescend to look in the book, but corrects Reginald offhand. Plough would correct Æschylus himself just as coolly as he does Reginald; and in his heart firmly believes he can write far better grammar than that much bepraised tragic poet. The passage was one of those which has been entirely rewritten by Ploughs of different ages. German Ploughs and English and Irish Ploughs had alike had a finger in manu-

facturing the passage.   Nobody but a Plough
could make sense of it.   One of the negro melo-
dies might as well be called Æschylus as this
passage.   It was Plough's favourite passage.   He
considered it the finest in all ancient or modern
poetry.   Every Plough had a peculiar reading of
his own; and our Plough's was perhaps the worst
of all.   The German Plough, who edited the
edition Reginald held in his hand, had by a
variety of conjectures, emendations, interpolations,
glosses, scholia, and elisions, botched up the famous
passage ; but no two Ploughs ever did agree upon
it ; and our Plough could by no means agree with
his German relative on any one point.   Every
reading was wrong; and Reginald found himself
amidst a bewildering variety of conjectures and
emendations.   This was Plough's famous Greek
conundrum.   If you once lost yourself in this
mist of words, once missed your road in this tragic
labyrinth of Greek particles, it was all over.
No help from Plough.   Did you think that was
some suggestion escaped his lips ?   That was the
emendation of some great Irish Plough.   If you

accept that you are irretrievably ruined. Poor
Reginald was fast on the road to grief. He had
accepted the great Irish Plough's emendation.

" If you read καὶ there "—for καὶ was the great
Irish Plough's emendation—" you must read καὶ
lower down, Mr. Neville-Aston;" and if you did
it would seem from Plough's speech that you
had far better have written Æschylus anew.
"*Davus sum non Œdipus*," at last Reginald said,
for he was becoming angry, and there seemed
every prospect of a scene ensuing over the famous
passage, when the junior proctor luckily made
his appearance, and Plough was obliged, much
to his sorrow, to relinquish the famous puzzle,
and content himself with setting Reginald on
some less obscure, and consequently far more
genuine passage of the old poet.

Amherst was examined by a good-natured, mild
old " Don."

" Thank you, Mr. Amherst," replied his examiner, after he had construed a short passage
of Sophocles; " I will not detain you any longer,"
and out he rushed, with a load off his heart.

26—2

"You are all safe," exclaimed his friends the boating men.

Presently Reginald made his appearance equally joyful, though very indignant at "that beast Plough." It was still early in the afternoon, and down they all went to the river for a "grind." The sun was shining bright and warm, for it was now late in May; the St. Matthew's barge had been fresh painted and gilded, and shone resplendent on the stream. The new " eight " had come down from London, and lay alongside like a long narrow coffin. The river was studded with one vast raft of boats. How little Bonnet steered through it was a mystery; not once had they to ship oars, though there was sometimes scarcely an inch to spare. They shot down the river, passing pair-oars, and punts, and dinkies, and sailing craft, every one of them crowding away in shore as the St. Matthew's eight neared. How the new boat went, was the theme of every one when they reached Iffley, for the "schools" were forgotten. She had been built under the eye of the St. Matthew's captain, who during the

Easter vacation passed most of his time in the boat-yard of the great Mr. Skiffe, of Lambeth. But they must be back again to see whether the *testamurs* are out.

"Let us put on a spirt home," cried Lascelles, as they reached "the Willows;" and away went the St. Matthew's eight dashing through the water like some sword-fish; and not till little Bonnet cried "easy all," was the pace slackened, when he drew her alongside of their barge, where a party of St. Matthew's men were standing watching its progress.

"*Testamurs* out!" cried Reginald.

"No, not yet," is the reply.

"We will see to them," said Lascelles; "you won't surely go yourself."

But Reginald will; and away he goes with all the eight into the school's quad.

Five o'clock in Oxford; boating men are streaming up from the river; reading men returning from walking; lounging men sauntering from one another's rooms; riding men dismounting their horses, and the bells of every college pealing for dinner. Five o'clock, and the *testamurs* not yet out! The clerk of the " schools," looking like the infinitesimal part of an examiner —he has by constant attendance contracted quite an examinational look—blocks up the doorway. It is a strange scene; friends waiting for friends' *testamurs*, sometimes a father waiting for a son's. Half-past five, and no *testamurs* still out.

Let us take a look at this school's quad, where so many a man has paced up and down waiting in agony. A black swarm of caps and gowns is crowding round that narrow archway guarded by the official Cerberus. Little knots of men are standing in twos or threes, constantly untying themselves, and then walking restlessly up and down. But there is some one walking alone : it is that poor lady waiting for her husband's *testamur*. Every moment she looks anxiously round to that narrow doorway. The St. Matthew's eight, whose white flannel trousers contrast strangely with ·the black gowns, are becoming impatient, and condemning Plough in no measured terms. Six o'clock, and no *testamurs* out! Reginald, who had felt so certain, was beginning to have fears, that at this moment the examiners might be holding an inquest upon his papers, that Plough had discovered some mistake, and refused to sign his *testamur*. Even you, my dear reader, who, I have no doubt, are a brilliant Greek and Hebrew scholar, have perhaps experienced these misgivings. If you have not, I know many eminent friends of mine who have. At last come the examiners, meek and mild. Who would ever think that yon milk-sop was Plough, the terrible examiner? Out of the schools he is nothing. Men rush to the door; the clerk of the "schools" can hardly stand the siege. It is a wonder those bits of paper are not torn to pieces in the scramble.

"Hurrah! here are yours, Neville and Amherst," shouted Lascelles.

They have all passed. All? No; there is one not though. That lady walking in the dim, dark shadow of the Bodleian, herself a shadow, will come up timidly when all the men have gone away, and ask in vain for her husband's *testamur*.

But Reginald has never yet caught a glimpse of that document where he will behold Plough's valuable autograph, and half doubts if it is in existence. " Who has Neville's *testamur* ?" but it cannot be found, for some kind friend has run wildly off with it to his rooms, not knowing he was so near. He read and re-read that little piece of paper to make quite sure, as thousands have done before him, and tips his scout, who seems to share the honours of the day. That night Reginald gives a " wine:" the whole college nearly is there. Pogis and Slowcombe have sent twice to stop the noise. " Three cheers for the St. Matthew's eight !" " Three cheers for the St. Matthew's *Torpid !* " " Three cheers for the St. Matthew's eleven ! " ring again through the quad. Lights burn in candlesticks of every description ; wine sparkles—not Oxford wine, for it never did such a thing—in decanters of all sizes and glasses of all shapes, for his scout has made a raid upon all the china and glass in the college. Crimp, the pastry-cook, has sent in a double amount of dessert. Song rattles after song ; boating men, hunting, cricketing men, tufts and commoners and scholars all mixed together in a thick mist of tobacco-smoke. Merrily trolls forth that old university chorus, "For he's a jolly good fellow."

Reginald hears it applied to himself, and for the first time in his life has to return thanks. But the party is breaking; a few linger, and they too are gone. Reginald jumps into bed, and awakes the next morning with a slight headache. His rooms look like most rooms after a "wine." Broken pipes, half-burnt weeds, and orange-peel, and tobacco tessellate the floor, and the table is veneered with wine-stains; a few broken glasses and plates, many empty decanters and bottles meet the eye. Reginald comes back from chapel; his room is in order, and nothing but a stronger smell of tobacco than usual prevades it. Nothing else? Some day Crimp's bill will appear; but for Crimp and his bills Reginald cares nothing just now.

CHAPTER IX.

THE GREAT BOAT-RACE.

AND now everything in Oxford was wearing its brightest and best appearance. The St. Matthew's garden was bursting into full splendour. There you might see on the lawn a party of young exquisites, friends most of them of Alfred Craven's, practising archery in the afternoons, or some of the reading men playing quietly at bowls. Strange contrast between those two sets! Aristotle, it is said, was a fop. I wonder what he would have thought of some of these reading-men in their coats made by country tailors, and their boots by village cobblers, compared with the handsome young Lord Belvidere who has just put an arrow into the gold. Why, that cambric shirt which Alfred Craven wears, with

its magnificent front, cost all poor Jones's wardrobe put together.

Down upon the river fleets of " eights " were
racing might and main to Iffley; men racing
down by their sides timing them; shouts of coxswains, shouts of men in pair-oars, dinkies,
and punts: the blue water lashed and beaten
with the oars into endless little ripples and eddies.
The St. Matthew's " eight " stand upon their barge
watching the St. Mark's boat shoot by with its
flashing wings; but they, too, are soon seated in
that narrow plank of theirs, which they call their
" eight," and are as proud of as of any of
England's noblest vessels. Along they race, little
Bonnet cutting every corner, saving every inch.
Up the stream they pull again, flying past the
" Long Bridges," and " the Willows," so that
it might be said of their boat, as Reginald
remarked,—

" Et fugit ad salices, sed se cupit ante videri ; "

and they determined it should be seen first.
Evening after evening do they practise. Lascelles, the captain, comes round every night to

see they are in bed by ten. No smoking, no beer-drinking, no wine parties.

And now the first night of the races had come. The banks of the river swarm with men, the punts can scarcely take them across. The St. Matthew's boat is down in good time. What a distance it seems between them and the place where the St. Mark's boat will be, and yet how short that between them and St. Luke's! Eights come quickly down, one after another, and take their places. The St. Mark's is coming, and now they are turning their boat like a long huge canoe. All St. Matthew's is congregated round its "eight." The Dons have come down. Pogis and Slowcombe are actually there. The scouts of St. Matthew's are down. The whole Cadeocracy of Oxford is there, for St. Matthew's is a favourite college with that portion of the populace who run their errands, look after their dogs, and take their horses from the college gate to Tandem's and Ippus's. Up and down the banks the crews are walking in their boating coats, like race-horses in cloths and rugs before they start. The first

gun has sounded, men are strolling on to the
"Long Bridges," and the crews are stripping.
Fine tall fellows were the St. Matthew's crew.
It is a wonder that shell of a boat can bear their
weight. There was Rollock looking like an
amateur prize-fighter, if you can imagine such
a being as an intellectual-looking prize-fighter;
Lascelles, the captain, with his handsome face,
Grenville standing six feet two, and pulling number six, Cleveland nearly as tall, Walter Merry,
and Rushout, and Sinclair, and Reginald Neville
the finest of them all. The second gun! and
they are out on the stream as far as the painter,
which little Bonnet holds, will allow. Men on
the banks are counting the seconds. "Now, then,
be ready!" Reginald's feet are firm against the
stretcher. Another second, and they hear the
roar of the gun, accompanied by the roar of the
men on the banks. The first few strokes Reginald scarcely takes. Now he feels the swing of
the boat. She quivers with the speed. Still the
din on the banks thunders. They are already
past the "Long Bridges." On the far side of

the river they shoot. Now they cross. The
sounds of voices roar louder. "You are gaining,"
"Now, then, put it on." The boat seems flying.
Men cheer them. "You are gaining; you are
gaining fast." They strain to the utmost. It is
of no use. They were only two yards behind.
But they could not make them up.

Men are crossing the river in puntfuls, talking
how St. George's bumped St. Luke's, and how
St. Winipeg's ran into the bank. Night after
night this wild pursuit takes place. Once St.
Matthew's actually overlapped St. Mark's; once
it lost one of its oars, and was all but bumped
by St. George's. So still St. Mark's was head
of the river.

To-night is the last of the races. If a bump
is made it is now or never. All Oxford is
centered upon those two boats. Even Hicks and
Jones are in a state of enthusiasm. To-night
the banks are lined on both sides. A laden barge
is slowly crawling up the stream amidst various
anathemas. "Only make a good start, and you
are sure to do it," every one said. The St. Mat-

thew's boat has never yet got off well, for it is on an awkward bend of the river, whilst the St. Mark's boat is on a straight piece. To-night there are country clergymen up from out-of-the-way livings and wild curacies; you can tell them at once. "Eights" are coming down to their stations. There is St. Winipeg's with its crew all in white, looking like amateur millers; and there comes St. Greenacre's, with its men in long blue jerseys, looking like butcher boys; and there goes St. David's, the great Welsh college, with its crew of Joneses, with a green leek in their caps, and a goat, playing a harp, rampant on their vests. The first gun has sounded, scattering the men in all directions, as if it had been loaded with grape. All the best points down the river have been secured, but the occupants will never be able to keep them. As far as the eye can reach, up to Folly Bridge itself, a human wall fringes the river. Several false alarms have been given, though the second gun has not yet gone. And now it goes. Men are mad with excitement. They are counting the seconds on the bank. "Now be ready!" and they start with the flash of the gun. The boat goes more like a piece of iron machinery driven by steam than by human arms. Reginald sees nothing, feels nothing, hears nothing, though the very banks and bridges thunder with a thousand voices. Like two long snakes seem those boats in this fierce pursuit, the water hissing at their bows. The pace increases. And now the St. Matthew's boat rocks and heaves as if caught in a mill-race. The crew know what it means, and pull as if for life itself.

"Now then, put it on!" cries little Bonnet, and they make their last spirt.

The blue water swirls by them. It is a long and desperate struggle. With set teeth and clenched arms they drive the boat through the surf. "A bump! a bump!" is thundered from the banks; but not yet do they cease, and not until little Bonnet stands up waving his cap do the men feel certain of victory. And Reginald looks up and sees confusion on the shore, and men trampled on, and pushed ankle-deep and knee-deep in the water, and amid the cheers of friends and the sounds of music they pulled slowly to their barge. The cabin is full of noise, remarks on the race, questions asked, bets paid. A few hours later, and Reginald is at one of the largest boat suppers St. Matthew's ever saw. The old college walls rock with the noise. No " Dons " interfere, for they are as proud—some o them, at least—as the " eight " themselves of the victory.

CHAPTER X.

COMMEMORATION AT OXFORD.

THIS year it was what is called a grand commemoration, that is, two or three ordinary commemorations rolled into one. Mrs. Neville had promised to come up if she could obtain Mr. Aston Neville's consent. "Lionesses" of all kinds were pouring into Oxford, "lionesses" fierce as the genuine animal, "lionesses" mild and tame. At last Reginald hears from Mr. Aston Neville, and has orders to engage lodgings. Lectures are all over, collections over, and the Saturnalia of Oxford begun. And now that Mr. Aston Neville has come, he cannot stay, for he is wanted on some railway committee in the House.

"Why, your Oxford friends are like some sheep we once saw in the Highlands; they come close

up and stare at you, as if they had never seen
a human face before," said Minnie, and she is
pretty correct.

Reginald has leave from the common-room to
have some of the college plate, for luncheon; and
Lascelles has allowed him the use of various claret
jugs and goblets, won at various races, all of which
his scout William is arranging on the table to
the astonishment of Mrs. Neville.   Men come up
to his rooms on various pretexts, merely to catch
a glimpse of Miss Minnie, the fame of whose
beauty had already gone through St. Matthew's.
William, the scout, said, that, all the time he had
been in the college, he had never seen so pretty
a young lady as Miss Neville.   But William's
opinion ought not to be of much weight, for he
was in the habit of making this assertion in refer-
ence to the sisters of all his masters.

"Oh, I beg pardon, I did not know you had
any one here," cried Amherst, as he entered,
and was for making a hasty retreat, which Reginald prevented.

"Let me introduce my friend, Mr. Amherst,

27—2

to you, cousins Lucy and Minnie, of whom you
have heard me speak so much."

Mrs. Neville began asking Amherst about the
college plate with its wonderful Latin inscriptions.

"This is like some Arabian romance," said
Miss Minnie: "here was Reginald this morning
did not possess even a kettle or a toasting-fork,
and now has his table laden with all this
silver."

The college system of lending, and consequently
losing, which terms at Oxford are synonymous,
Mrs. Neville did not understand.

"We have to thank you for your kettle,
Mr. Amherst, I think," said Minnie.

"I wanted Reginald to have it sent back,"
continued Mrs. Neville.

"But the fact is," Reginald replied, "the kettle
is really mine, Amherst, I believe."

Amherst assented, and explained that he and
Reginald were in partnership, as far as kettles,
corkscrews, toasting-forks, and the like were
concerned. And Minnie thought the firm could

not be in a very flourishing condition, when it possessed only one very black kettle, and a toasting-fork like an ancient javelin, with only one prong. Nor was the crockery of the firm highly approved.

"You see, Amherst, they live close to the potteries, in the cup and saucer land, in a region of plates, in the district of dishes; and our seeming poverty alarms them," Reginald replied.

"I know," said Miss Minnie, "I had a cup of one pattern, a saucer of another, and a plate of a third, and that the tea-cups were of different sizes and shapes, and had to do duty for coffee-cups."

"Oh, yes," said Reginald, "that is very natural. Amherst and I have joined our stock of china together, and we call them the senior and junior united services."

Whether it was this joke of Reginald's, or the pitiable condition of the plates and cup, saffected Mrs. Neville, is not known, but she promised to present the firm with a new breakfast service, which came up early next term. In with Amherst

had come two or three hairy Scotch terriers, who
had subscription kennels in various coal-boxes and
cupboards.

" You seem, though, to have a complete menagerie of dogs in the college," said Minnie; " I
saw two or three looking out a window in the
' quad,' as you call it.   Do you keep any cats as
well ? "

" Oh, no !" said Amherst.

" I should think not," said Reginald; " we have
the greatest authority against such a proceeding,
for we read in Horace of *Rupili pus atque venenum ;*
don't we, Amherst ? "

At this moment Alfred Craven entered, and
Minnie begged him to explain the Latin sentence,
which confused him to a great extent.   William
followed bringing the best lunch Cutlets, the
St. Matthew's cook, could devise.   There was of
course the great college tankard filled with cider-
cup, into which Minnie just dipped those ruby
lips of hers, as if to cool them, and which poor
little Flo could scarcely lift up to her mouth.
There were also Reginald's pewters, which he had

won at various pair-oar and "scratch" races, and
the vases and cups the St. Matthew's boat had
carried off at different regattas. All these had
one considerable advantage, in the eyes of ladies,
over the college plate—the inscriptions were all
written in English. Miss Minnie in her wicked
way wished to know how many pewters Alfred
Craven possessed; she might as well have asked
him how many University prizes he had taken.
Luncheon over, and away they set " to do " the
sights of rare old Oxford. No " lioness " ever
laughed so much as Minnie did that fine June
afternoon.

"My dear lioness, don't roar quite so loud;
we are in the Bodleian, remember, and we shall
have the librarian after us in a minute," said
Reginald.

They went all over Oxford ; seedy touters
and guides offered their assistance, but Reginald
and Amherst knew Oxford better than any guide.
They saw the famous chapel of St. Winipeg's,
and the cloisters of St. Gridiron's: the museum
of St. George's, and the hall of St. Boniface,

and the gardens of St. Mark's and Luke's.
Minnie was in her highest spirits and her best
looks. Her eyes sparkled, and that pretty pink
dress suited her. All "lionesses" seemed so many
tame cats compared to her. They met Jones
walking with his sister, who seemed like some
stunted charity girl beside the tall, handsome
Minnie. But not the Hickses and the Joneses
alone were so inferior; there was Lord Belvidere
and his party, whom they saw in the cloisters
of St. Gridiron's; why, Lord Belvidere's sister
looks only like a poor painted doll to Minnie.

"Dinner-time! impossible!" cried Mrs. Neville.

"Why, you do nothing else but eat, in Oxford," was Minnie's remark.

And I have known, as I dare say the reader
has, other less sagacious "lionesses" say the same
thing.

"You are going to dine in hall to-day," said
Reginald.

Mrs. Neville at first objected, but was persuaded by Minnie.

"We must go to our lodgings first," continued

Minnie; "for I must smooth my hair; unless"
—this in a whisper—"the firm can lend me a
hairbrush."

So they go back to St. Matthew's, little Flo
nearly tripping over the entrance door-sill. Dinner is to-day at four, so that there may be time
to see the boat procession in the evening. The
bell has already gone, and Minnie finishes brushing her long glossy hair, and again readjusts
that charming pink bonnet. They cross the deserted "quad," for every one has gone into dinner.
Reginald had applied to the bursar for seats,
and the common-room man comes to him to say
that four places have been kept for them at the
high table. The St. Matthew's dining-hall is
very long, only exceeded in length by the Latin
grace which precedes every dinner, as Minnie
observed on another occasion, when they were
in time for that ceremony. Reginald had never
sat at the high table before, and found himself
next to Pogis. Minnie's neighbour is Lord Belvidere, who is very attentive to her, more so
than to his cousin, who is slightly red-haired.

The old hall looks gay and bright; flowers
are in all the windows, and the old founders
and benefactors smile down upon the guests from
their bright gilt frames.   There are a good many
" lionesses " at all the tables ; some of them, I am
compelled to say, resembling the real animal
only in their method of eating.   It has been
often remarked that when " Dons " have a mind to
be grand, no men can be more so.   To-day the
entertainment is most extensive; St. Matthew's
had been doing great things, and the " Dons "
were well pleased.   One man had taken a first
class; and one of the bachelors had carried off
the Latin essay, and a great number of scholars
and commoners—at least one-third of the college,
all who could rhyme, in fact, and a great number
who could not—had not carried off the Newdigate; but greatest of all, in the estimation of a
certain small table in the middle of the hall,
they were head of the river.   Pogis did not
wear those brilliant studs, and a gown that
would have done credit to any court milliner
in London, for nothing; nor the rector sit at

the end of the table in that alarming scarlet
robe for nothing.

"Now, Reginald, do take care, and do not
drink quite so much wine," Mrs. Neville whispers, as Reginald is continually asked by various
friends. Even Pogis asks him. Every one
seems happy. There is a colour even upon the
yellow vellum face of Pogis, and the chalky out-
lines of Slowcombe's cheeks; perhaps, though,
it was only the reflection of the rector's scarlet
robes. But happiest of all do the boating-men
seem. Lascelles has his two sisters up, and
Granville his cousins; and that girl with the
beautiful eyes is engaged to Rushout. The
magnanimous "Dons" have given a general invitation to every one who has ladies to the common-room. Pogis is pressing Reginald, who re-
fers him to Mrs. Neville. Pogis actually, too,
talks about the boats, but cannot help quoting a
description of a boat-race from Virgil, the only
one he knows anything about. Dinner over,
and grace said in Latin, during which all the
"lionesses" looked particularly pious and knowing,

and they adjourn to the St. Matthew's common-room. A long, low room is this St. Matthew's common-room; looking out upon the " Dons' " garden, where dessert is carried out by the scouts. A strange little garden is this, where Pogis generally reads Aristotle, but where he is now so busy asking Miss Minnie to have some pine-apple. The grass-plat is green and fresh, and the old college walls are dyed with golden lichens, and here and there silvered with a mosaic work of moss. Reginald introduced Pogis to Minnie, at his especial request. How the rogue smirked and blushed at first! But he knows a pretty girl. Latin and Greek have not knocked that perception out of him.

" Isn't this capital claret, Neville? " said Lascelles, as the scout comes round with the claret jug. " How the ' Dons ' are doing the thing ! I say, do you see Pogis is sweet upon the pretty cousin ? "

Mrs. Neville at this moment approached, on her way to detach Miss Minnie from Pogis. But Pogis was not so easily to be detached.

COMMEMORATION AT OXFORD.   141

He followed Mrs. Neville and Minnie most per-
tinaciously round the garden.   He was evidently
smitten with Minnie.   " The affair might be
serious with any one else, but is simply ludi-
crous in Pogis's case," said Reginald to himself.

Pogis was like a little shrivelled piece of vellum
beside that tall handsome girl, who swept the
grass so stately with that pink dress.

" Come, Regy, give me your arm, and we
will go," said Mrs. Neville, and they left poor
Pogis looking very disconsolate.   Miss Minnie
was, I am sorry to say, rather sarcastic upon
Pogis.

" He does not drink champagne every day,
Minnie, you must know," Reginald said, by way
of excuse; but that young lady still kept up an
amusing commentary on his conversation.

" I must leave you at your lodgings, whilst I
put on my boating things," said Reginald.   Mrs.
Neville was a little tired after the day's exploits, and
was glad to have an hour's rest.   Flo, too, com-
plained of being a little, only a little though, tired;
but Miss Minnie was as lively as ever.   When

Reginald reached college every one was talking about Pogis's evident attachment to the pretty cousin.

"He was quite discomfited after you left," said Lascelles, "and looked the picture of despair." As Pogis ordinarily had that appearance, Reginald was not much alarmed concerning him. "I left him drinking bumpers of claret, as if to drown his sorrow;" this was far more alarming news, and Reginald trembled for Pogis's safety. He put on his boating things, found Alfred Craven, and was off to the lodgings in the "High." Mrs. Neville had had a good rest, and little Flo declares she is not at all tired. If Minnie was, she would not say so, but she does not at all look like it.

"Come, let me look at your jersey," she said, unbuttoning Reginald's thick boating coat which just revealed part of the blue St. Matthew's mitre, which attracted her attention. The St. Matthew's jersey was the admiration of all "lionesses," and Miss Minnie declared a most favourable opinion upon it, and also admired the straw hat with the blue and white ribbons, and even the thick boat-

ing coat; perhaps she so studiously praised the
coarse boating coat to vex Alfred Craven, who
wore the most dandified glossy coat the famous
Oxford tailors, Flannel and Vesey, could build.

All Oxford was streaming down to the river:
"Dons" and "lionesses;" sleek Oxford tradesmen
with their wives and pretty daughters.   Flags are
flying in all directions; but above them all high
on the University barge the eagle of St. Matthew
is spreading its blue and golden wings in the
setting sun.   The band is playing.   All is life
and animation.   They have reached the St.
Matthew's barge, which looks like the galley in
which Antony and Cleopatra sailed up the Nile,
and Miss Minnie begins quoting—

> "The poop is beaten gold,
> Purple the sails."

But, as Reginald informed her, it was in reality
only an old lord mayor's barge, which had been
bought secondhand and regilded.

"Now be careful over the plank," said Reginald;
but Miss Minnie is across it, to the astonishment

of Alfred Craven, who trembles as if he were walking it in another sense.

The St. Matthew's barge is crowded with "lion- esses," a perfect menagerie of them. Lascelles' party is there, and those tall girls in white are Granville's cousins. Reginald is turning away when he sees poor Hicks and his sister, and Jones and his sister, struggling vainly in the crowd on shore. Miss Hicks stands somewhere about four feet in her thick shoes; and in her present position might as well be a hundred miles away, as far as seeing anything upon the river. Jones and Hicks would no more venture upon the St. Matthew's barge, than their sisters into an outrigger.

"Come, Hicks and Jones, I will put your sisters in a good place, if you will allow me," cried Reginald. Every seat but one is engaged. He places little Miss Jones in it. What is he to do with Miss Hicks, who apparently wears a pair of worsted stockings for gloves with extem- porary finger-stalls, and a bonnet made from an old gingham umbrella? He leans over to Minnie, who occupies one of the front seats, and asks her to make room, which she does, sadly crumpling that pink dress of hers. "Now, Miss Hicks, if you please," and he passes that young lady over with the worsted-stocking gloves, one of which nearly comes off in his hands.

"Stop a minute, Regy, and tell me the names of the boats which pass, for Alfred Craven does not know them," said Minnie.

"Here comes our *Torpid*, I see," answered Reginald, and as he spoke they could hear the regular sharp stroke of the oars, like the noise a bird makes when it first flies from its starting-place.

"Oh, how pretty!" exclaim all the "lionesses," as the blue glancing oars dip into the blue stream, and the water drops off them like golden dew in the setting sun. "Eights" follow now in quick succession and much confusion.

"Do stop and tell me their names," again begs Minnie.

"Here is a chart and key to all the boats, flags, and dresses," replied Reginald, handing her "the

correct card of the races." And a few minutes
after, as the St. Matthew's "eight" comes dashing
by, he sees Minnie and the little girl with the
umbrella bonnet both studying it.

Minnie looks up and smiles at Reginald, and
is proud to see him pulling, and to point him out
to little Miss Hicks; and little Flo claps her
hands with delight. "If the lionesses thought
so much of our *Torpid*, what can they think of
our 'eight'?" thought Reginald to himself, for
he was rather conceited on this subject. But
lionesses do not distinguish between "eights" and
Torpids, and most of them thought it was the
same boat which they had seen before. And now
the St. Matthew's boat took up its position. The
"eights" are coming up to salute it. First comes
their old rival, the St. Mark's, with their golden
lion at the bow. They give them a right good
hearty cheer. Then comes St. Laurence's, with
its white flag and the gridirons on it, and all the
men with gridirons on their breasts. And in
quick succession follow St. George's, and St.
Luke's, and St. Barnacle's with much confusion,

for St. Laurence's can't turn, and the nose of St.
Barnacle's has unshipped the rudder of St. Ur-
sula's, and coxswains are shouting to coxswains,
and oars are hopelessly entangled with oars, and the
lionesses think it all very beautiful. And now
comes the St. Matthew's *Torpid*. What a cheer
their "eight" gives them! it rings up and down
the river. Once more and once more again, and
they cheer them again and again as they pass.
And now come the other *Torpids* in worse
confusion than the "eights," and the "lionesses"
are more pleased than ever. The oars go up one
by one, like the arms of a windmill, never two
up at the same time.

"Just what I expected," cried Reginald, as
the St. Winipeg's *Torpid* went over. The "lionesses" scream and go into convulsions, but the
water is not very deep. Punts put out in all
directions. The spirit of the Humane Society
is in all the Oxford boatmen—it is in boatmen
of all sorts when they know the water is not very
deep. And now it is all over. The St. Matthew's
"eight" pull to their own barge, and lie along-

side. Reginald finds Minnie and the little girl
of the brown gingham umbrella bonnet very good
friends. "Lionesses" peep timidly down into that
thing like a long, hollow bamboo split horizontally
which is called the St. Matthew's "eight." Reginald steps out, and Minnie takes his arm. Alfred
Craven brings up the rear with Mrs. Neville
and little Flo. They wander round the meadows
till late. The stars are peeping out over the
tall elms. The Cherwell looks like some creek
in the river, rather than a separate stream. Silence is on the river and in the barges, where
but an hour ago all was confusion, merriment, and
life.

When Reginald reached college, he found a
card from Pogis inviting his cousins and himself to
breakfast next morning,

"I should like to have gone," said Minnie,
when she saw Pogis's neat little card with his
copper-plate handwriting, which you can scarcely
distinguish from his printed name; but Mrs. Neville was of opinion it would never have done;
so they enjoy a quiet little breakfast in Regi-

nald's rooms, and eat plenty of Oxford straw-
berries.

To-day they have tickets for the theatre, and
must go in good time. " Lionesses " now are being
torn in hot haste through the school's quad.   Men
are besieging the undergraduates' entrance.

" I can go no farther with you, cousin Lucy;
you must now fight your own way," said Reginald; which Miss Minnie will do very well, and
very stately.   It is said that you see human nature behind the scenes of an ordinary theatre;
perhaps so, but it is not the best part.   Certainly
you see it to-day at this Oxford theatre.   Who
would think that those gentle-looking ladies in silks
and satins and gauze would ever race and push
in that mad way!   Those " lionesses " are far worse
than the throng of black caps and gowns, which is
besieging the undergraduates' entrance.   Now the
gates are open, and the men rush up that narrow
winding staircase, Reginald leading the van.   The
gallery is already full, men swarming in the windows like so many big black flies, and resting on
the ledges like so many big black bats.   A terri-

ble critic is this mob in the gallery. Like all other mobs, it has its favourites, but it is more keen-witted than any other mob. Plough is just coming in with a party of ladies, and his entrance is the signal for a storm of hisses. Nemesis sits to-day enthroned in the undergraduates' gallery. Hiss follows hiss like water falling upon hot iron. In vain the vice-chancellor attempts to open the proceedings. No one shall be heard, unless Plough is turned out. The vice-chancellor in vain turns imploring eyes to that gallery, which shows a bit, and a good bit too, of its unmistakeable mind. Will not nature exhaust itself? Undergraduate nature is not so easily exhausted. The cries are louder, fiercer than ever. The very gallery shakes, and "lionesses" are in dread, when Plough suddenly retreats. The storm has ceased. The clouds have passed away from the undergraduate mind; cheers for favourites follow; cheers for the ladies in general; then cheers for ladies in particular; cheers for ladies in blue, and ladies in pink; and ladies in pink and blue all blush, each thinking that she is the one most particularly

admired. This, though, is too bad, to individual-
ize, so distinctly. "Three cheers for the lady in
the pink bonnet near a pillar in the front row."
Every one looks, and it turns out to be Miss
Minnie, who is the only lady in a pink bonnet
near a pillar in the front row, and who is blushing
excessively, which does not at all decrease her
beauty.

And now, after various Latin speeches, which
sounded all pretty much alike to the "lionesses,"
and reminded them of nothing they had ever heard
except the long Latin grace at yesterday's feast,
and when the vice-chancellor had conferred all the
honorary degrees, Block of St. Winipeg's recited
his refreshing poem on the Niger, or Timbuc-
too, or the Nile. I think it was that year, from a
cry of *nil admirari* in the gallery, which greeted
its commencement, and sounded very like Reginald's voice: and every man who had sent in a
poem, that is to say, one-half of the mob in the
gallery, thought theirs decidedly better than
Block's, whilst the other half vehemently cheered
the delighted Block, reciting away to the "lion-

esses," who now really welcomed anything in
English—even an Oxford Newdigate. And now
Block is drawing to a conclusion. Starlight, and
sunlight, and moonlight, and the light of rubies
and diamonds, he has long ago exhausted; and
if the reader would like to know how Block concluded, he had better buy any Oxford prize poem
which has been published within the last fifty years,
for Newdigates have all one ending, and for that
matter one beginning and one middle. And now
the brilliant composition was finished, and the poet
was lost to the admiring gaze of lionesses; and
lionesses, as soon as they were out of the building,
were buying Block of St. Winipeg's poem on the
Nile, which Reginald found Minnie busy reading
in his rooms. I should not have liked Block to
have seen the criticisms on the margin which this
fair Gifford had been making. Lord Belvidere's
sister declared to Reginald at dinner, that it was
the sweetest poem she had ever read; which
verdict did not give him a very high opinion of
her ladyship's literary abilities.

To-morrow again there is more recitation and

honorary degrees, but Mrs. Neville and Minnie
do not care to go.   Yet there are "lionesses" who
would give their ears and their tails to go both
days: so Reginald sends his tickets to little Miss
Hicks, whom he did not see there yesterday,
for Hicks, poor fellow, has no friends at court;
and the cousins gallop off to Blenheim.

"How very lucky we brought our riding
habits!" said Minnie, in her most artless way;
but there was very little luck in the matter, for
Minnie had with great care seen them herself
packed up.

Minnie goes with Reginald down to Tandem's
stables: Mrs. Tandem has a favourite mare, very
quiet, which will just suit Mrs. Neville, and Tandem allows them to have his daughter's pony for
little Flo, for Reginald, on the whole, is a pretty
good customer to him, and St. Matthew's divides
its favours very fairly between him and Ippus.
Amherst and Alfred Craven are of the party.

"My dear Regy, it will never do to keep the
high road; I thought you once told me this was
never done at Oxford, that high roads were only

for carriages and reading men," said Minnie, after they had gone some two miles on the turnpike road.

" Wait a little, you surely will not ride into the standing corn; we shall come into a grazing country in a minute," Reginald replied.

So they turned into the first grass field.

"Come along, Mr. Amherst," said Minnie, who quickly followed; but Alfred Craven declined, either out of gallantry to Mrs. Neville, or because he knew Minnie's style of riding.

Oxfordshire farmers, instead of becoming reconciled to that one great law of habit, which is often said to be synonymous with second nature, are the most impatient of it.

" I wonder they do not become used to this sort of thing," said Minnie, as they perceived a farmer and his men coming after them armed with pitchforks, for Oxfordshire farmers have a great and unconquerable aversion to men riding over their fields and fences; and every time it is done, instead of becoming used to it, have a greater dislike to the proceeding.

· " Do you think you can take the hedge, Minnie ? " cried Reginald.

" I mean to try," was her answer.

There was no time to be lost, for by a short cut across the field the farmer and the men were close upon them. Up they came swearing and shouting, the old farmer hot with anger and the heat of the day.

Without hesitation Minnie rode at the hedge, but her horse refused.

" Good Lord ! " cried the farmer, whose anger was now turned into fear when he saw Miss Minnie's plan; " good Lord, don't ye do that; ye'll break your neck as sure as onything."

He had scarcely time to finish this wide-world comparison, when Miss Minnie was landed on the other side. Amherst had taken advantage of this slight diversion to elude the gaping plough-men, and was making for a pleached fence at the bottom, but Reginald crashed through the hedge and joined Minnie. They were now in a position to treat with the enemy, who were still rapt in admiration of Minnie's daring feat.

"Come, you know we have been trespassing after all," Minnie said; "and ought to make some amends."

But the farmer will take nothing; he gives them full leave to ride over his farm, which unfortunately very soon ends, and they think it not very prudent to venture on another, and so rejoin their party on the road, and narrate to them the tale of the Oxfordshire farmer, which occupies the time till they reach Blenheim. They see Blenheim as people see most "show-houses" in England, that is to say, not at all; but they have an excellent lunch at "The Bear and Ragged Staff;" they buy a great many pairs of Woodstock gloves, and are late again for dinner; and the whole hall stares at Miss Minnie in the pink bonnet, and knows it is the same which was so cheered in the theatre.

And now, ye Muses, give me a ruby-nibbed pen, and violet-coloured ink, and paper of the creamiest complexion; for this stump of a pen, this black thick ink, can never describe on common foolscap the glories of a University ball. O

Block, sweet poet of St. Winipeg's! help me to relate the dress which Lady Bayswater wore, and the wreath which the Countess of Tintack had in her hair, and that charming head-dress of Lady Bonnibel. All the diamonds and rubies which were in Block's poem yesterday morning were at the University ball to-night. The gentlemen on whom honorary degrees had been conferred were there, looking none the worse for that ceremony. Heads of colleges and their awful-looking wives were there. That gouty old fellow is the head of St. Winipeg's, and that's his wife, in the black satin, between her two daughters. She is trying to catch young Lord Vanillas, who is now at St. Winipeg's, for one of them. Lord Vanillas was only the Honourable Mr. Sleightone when he first came up to college, and but lately, by the sudden death of his elder brother, came to the title, and consequently wonderfully increased in the estimation of the rectoress of St. Winipeg's. He is dancing just now with Miss Minnie, to whom Reginald introduced him. There actually is Pogis; he knows the rectoress of St.

Winipeg's; she is asking him who is that waltzing with Lord Vanillas. Minnie has so many
partners she hardly knows what to do. Pogis
is hauking round the room after her; he dare
not pounce upon her, for she is now talking to
the Countess of Bayswater. Now she is moving
away to join Mrs. Neville, and Pogis bears down
upon her. The next dance is the Lancers.

·. "I quite forgot I was engaged, Mr. Amherst,"
Minnie says, when Amherst comes to claim her
as his partner, and she takes Pogis's arm.

"What methodist parson is that with whom
Miss Neville is dancing?" says the Earl of
Bayswater to Lord Tintack; but Lord Tintack
has no conception, and merely says, "A monstrous
fine girl that!"

Any one who knows that delightful dance the
Lancers, can conceive the state of confusion
Pogis, who had never before attempted it,
would inevitably fall into. He had only asked
Minnie to dance a quadrille, but that young lady
assured him she was engaged for every dance
except a valse and the Lancers. Pogis knew a

valse was out of the question, and as to the
Lancers he knew nothing about them, save what
Minnie told him, that they were a quadrille, very
easy and simple. Pogis is soon in a state of
bewilderment; Reginald, who has long since become an accomplished dancer, happens to be in
the same set, and takes him by the shoulder, and
turns him the right way. Lord Rattan Rowe
looks through his eyeglass with mingled scorn
and pity at the poor wretch—the ladies regard
him as simply in the way—Miss Minnie dances
on as if nothing had occurred—the whole room
is laughing.

"By Jove, though, she has served the fellow
right," thought Reginald to himself, who had seen
Pogis persecuting her up and down the room.

And in this way was Pogis cured of his love
for Minnie. The poor fellow sneaked out of the
room as soon as the Lancers were over. I dare
say Pogis knew all about the Pyrrhic dance, but
of the Lancers he was certainly ignorant. So the
night rattled on: Mr. Aston Neville was expected
down by the last train, but had not appeared.

Morning is breaking, and Mrs. Neville proposes going, but Minnie cannot yet possibly leave. There she goes with Reginald, whirling along in that white dress of hers, light as a flake of gossamer waltzing in the summer air. Every one admires her; all those famous men who had honorary degrees admire her. The Honourable Eli Barney, an American, admired her; and in an account of Oxford, in his recently published work of travels, makes especial mention of Miss Neville, with numerous particulars concerning her, interspersed with very valuable reflections.

"No Aston," said Mrs. Neville the next day at breakfast, expressing her sorrow at his absence. Reginald could not say he exactly sympathised with her. Mr. Aston Neville had now for a long time past been more engrossed in his semi-public affairs, and cared less for his wife and children. True, he had procured them tickets and cards at Oxford, but these are easily procurable, and no proof of affection. To-day Reginald had made arrangements for a boating party to Nuneham. Provisions had already gone down, and

were stored into a four oar, for Reginald and
Amherst had agreed, with the help of two Oxford
watermen, to pull the party down. How famously
they went, how Mrs. Neville begged of them
not to pull so hard, how little Flo and Alfred
Craven were frightened in the locks, how well
Minnie, after a little "coaching," steered, would
take too much space in this history to describe.
Cutlets, the St. Matthew's cook, had made
up two such plentiful hampers, that even with
the aid of the two Oxford boatmen, they could
not empty them. Mrs. Neville had promised to
provide the wine, and handed over to Reginald
all the Bushwood champagne she had brought
up with her. So underneath the trees of Nuneham Harcourt, might have been seen one of the
merriest picnics that ever were. Light-hearted
as the linnet in the elm-branches were they.
And Minnie poured forth her strains so sweetly,
that the very birds were hushed. Even Alfred
Craven has laid aside his languor. He forgets
even to drawl. Not even he, the greatest of
dandies, can be so affected, as to look at this green

grass and the fern with his eyeglass. Shawls have they, and plaids in all abundance; but, as Minnie says, who would use them when they may be seated on this green couch of moss? She has taken off her shawl and bonnet, and seems thoroughly to enjoy the blessed day.

" Come, Minnie, give us that song again," said Reginald; and she again sang it, and there was a sweetness about it, like the sound of falling waters to one who is jaded with city life in London. Little breezes came fanning their cheeks, pressing themselves, as if to be kissed, against their mouths. Along the ground shadows weave their warp and woof, patterned from the beach leaves. The two cousins stroll away under the trees; Minnie still without her bonnet, and her long hair falling down upon Reginald's shoulder. They have strayed from the rest. They have leisure to talk to themselves for the first time since they met in Oxford. Happy words, with but one alloy of grief, for they could not help seeing the black figure of Minnie's father standing upon Love's road, forbidding them to go forward. Yet happy minutes were they, only too swiftly-winged. They pace along slowly under the green aisles of the trees. The fern rustled against them, the moss grew greener with every dent their feet made on it. It was deep, true love they felt, as their lips pressed together. But they must be returning, and they did not loosen their hands until they came close to the rest. Minnie puts on her bonnet, and though she requires no aid, asks Reginald to help her; and though she knows he can't tie a bow, lets him fasten those two pink ribbons beneath that white warm chin of hers. But they must leave, for it will take some time to row home against the stream. It is quite dark when they reach Iffley; the water comes rushing into that long well of a lock, bubbling and boiling, and raising the boat up as with springs.

" My dear fellow, it is not the water that makes the boat rock, but your nervousness," said Reginald to the trembling Alfred Craven.

" Mr. Craven must, then, be very nervous," remarked the satirical Minnie, for the boat did roll not a little.

But the lock is nearly full; the water is again still; the lock-gates open, and they glide away. Lights are shining on Foley Bridge. And they see the black stacks and piles of colleges in the distance, and the outline of the Radcliffe, like a great black cloud brooding over the city.

CHAPTER XI.

MRS. NEVILLE'S SCHOOLS.

THE Oxford station was full of men going down;
men with sheaves of sticks and umbrellas; men
leading skye-terriers of all colours, pulling in
different directions, and refusing to enter their
travelling kennels; white-chokered "Dons," looking like a perplexed chorus in a Greek tragedy,
full of woes. "Lionesses," (how unlike those
"lionesses" of yesterday!) roaring like hyenas;
"lionesses'" luggage, consisting of many band-
boxes, and many bonnet-boxes; porters shouting,
"By your leave, sir;" and running over you; duns
hunting down their game. Such a crowd was
there in the Oxford station. Reginald manages to
collect the baggage of his party in safety, though
the lady's-maid will keep inquiring, "If missus has

her plaid shawl?" The porter is ringing a bell; the steam blowing off in a white cloud. The smooth metals glide under them. Little Flo is standing against the window counting the telegraph posts. Underneath bridges they fly, with little volleys of sound. Reginald is sitting next to Miss Minnie, and feels her arm entwined in his; Mrs. Neville is reading some book she purchased at the station-stall at Oxford. Into the dark gloom of tunnels, as at one stride into midnight itself, they plunge; and Reginald feels the arm press closer against him, and steals a long, silent kiss, drawn, as it were, from their very hearts. Over viaducts they fly, not seeming to touch them, but to jump from hill-side to hill-side. Past signal-men, whose white flags flutter in the breeze; by little sentry-boxes they shoot; and still ever did Reginald feel the warm and gentle pressure of that arm.

"Here is our station at last," cries little Flo.

Ah! little Flo, "at last," did you say? To Minnie and Reginald the time has gone too swiftly. The carriage was waiting, and Neptune,

the great Newfoundland dog, is on the platform,
looking most sagaciously at the train, with a
somewhat puzzled air, as much as to say, "This
is quite a new animal to me." They soon reached
Bushwood, little Flo taken up the whole way
with watching Nep, who quite disproved the
Latin verse, that man was the only animal that
looked upward, for Nep was gazing up to the
carriage all the way.

Reginald had his old study, and worked hard,
though not so hard as Mrs. Neville, who was
now toiling all day at her schools. Bushwood,
as has been said, lay immediately between the
potteries and the iron and coal districts. It was
in neither one nor the other, but a sort of
green oasis in the fiery desert of Ironshire. Close
to it, on both sides, little independent manufacturers and pit-owners were doing business on
a small scale, and employed amongst them a
good many "hands." The village of Bushwood
itself, the twenty or thirty houses that had the
boldness to call themselves a village, consisted
of an agricultural population, much in the same

state of ignorance as their fellows in various
parts of England; that is to say, only one in
six or seven could read or write, and that very
badly, and that one in virtue of this qualification
was commonly called "a scholard," and looked
upon as a sort of superior being. Upon the
children of these people Mrs. Neville first tried
her experiment. The scheme, however, had ex-
tended far beyond what she had originally con-
templated. The workpeople of these small pit-
owners and manufacturers, first one and then
another, begged to be allowed to send their children, whom Mrs. Neville was only too glad to
receive. Poor little Christian heathens! Nep.
knows more than they. Thank Heaven, there
are luckily in our England high-minded men
and women who will sacrifice both purse and
person to aid their poorer brethren. And Mrs.
Neville was one of these.

The schools were already again too small for
the children. It did not much matter this fine
summer weather, for they could learn their
lessons under the trees. But something must

be done for the winter-time. Mrs. Neville had
spent all her own available funds.   Old Mr.
Golding has come over to-day, and promised to
double his subscription; he knows very well that
Mrs. Neville's purse is tied up by her husband,
and adds—

"Now, my dear child, if you want any more,
don't for a moment hesitate to draw upon me."

But who is that tall, stout person, standing
with Mrs. Neville? Did you judge from his
dress, you would say a retired tradesman; from
his hands, which are rather big, a mechanic. It
was the Rev. Richard Benison, a true follower
of One, whom the old dramatist Decker has so
finely called,

> "The first true gentleman that ever breathed."

What, that person a clergyman without a
white choker! will exclaim the reader.   Some
ladies fancy white chokers make clergymen.   An
ordinary person, in fact very plain, is the Rev.
Mr. Benison.   His whiskers are like little
patches of red moss on the sides of his face.
His hair is entirely unconscious of Rowland's

Kalydor, if not of the more homely bear-grease.
Miss Minnie once sent him on his birthday a
present of a dressing-case, containing a looking-
glass. But the Rev. Mr. Benison's appearance
has not improved. Yet this is the incumbent
of the new church at Stoke Furnace; and, strange
to add, no pastor is so universally beloved. His
mind, too, some people would say, is as devoid
of all polish as his body. No soul for poetry
had Mr. Benison; and hence, perhaps, a defi-
ciency in that beautiful, florid style of preach-
ing, which just now is so fashionable; and by
which so many great reputations are achieved.
Place the Rev. Mr. Benison in one of the
fashionable churches of a fashionable watering-
place, and I think the beautiful Lady Bonnibel
would faint at one of his sermons. At Stoke
Furnace he was in his proper place. Plain, practical, matter-of-fact sermons did he preach; no
abstruse points; no millennial theories in them;
for the congregation were plain, practical people,
dealing daily with the stern realities of life,
fighting hard in all the hottest fire of this battle

of life. After hearing one of Benison's sermons, you could not tell whether he wore a gown or a surplice; and this is no small praise in these days.

Look at Mr. Benison's boots; they are so thick, and shod with iron, that you think he has had them made by mistake at the blacksmith's instead of the shoemaker's. Look how dirty they are; as if Warren, of blacking renown, had never existed. Nothing namby-pamby in the shake of his hands, but a firm, cordial greeting, as if the blood in his hand came direct by one straight vein from his heart. He does not stretch out two fingers to you, as Surplyce did once to Reginald, who asked him if he had hurt his remaining digits. You must not expect any witty impromptus from Mr. Benison, " he is not witty himself; " nor, on the other hand, " the cause of wit in others; " perhaps, on the contrary, he rather damps any great brilliancy in others. Miss Minnie is not so pert, and that glib little tongue of hers restrains itself, in his presence. What a world of kindness is there

in that soft hazel eye of his! With that eye,
though all his features are so plain, you cannot
call Mr. Benison ugly.

The school windows are open, and the door
is open, for it is a hot summer's morning. The
bee comes flying in; the swallow outside skims
up and down, and has one regular path in the
air, as though he had made a track. Come and
peep in at the door: two little children with
their arms round one another's necks, learning
from one book; a little boy on yonder stool
puzzling over a slate; Mrs. Neville explaining
the mysteries of the alphabet to a ragged class;
old Mr. Golding looking over wondrously formed
figures, which he constantly mistakes for the
wrong numbers; Miss Minnie setting a copy,
and a number of little things looking at her, as
though she were some professor of the black art;
Mr. Benison hearing a class read, whose blunders
would have discomposed anybody else's gravity.
So the time runs on, till they are suddenly surprised by hearing the hall clock chime out the
noon; and caps and bonnets are hastily put on,

and some hundred children are shouting and running on their way home.

"Won't you come to luncheon, Mr. Benison?" asks Mrs. Neville.

But he cannot stay, he is going back to Stoke Furnace to take a funeral, and cannot even accept Mrs. Neville's offer of a lift there in the carriage in the afternoon.

"If it was any one else but Mr. Benison, I should decidedly object to his interfering; but Mr. Benison's wish is not to give the Church power, but to do good," replied Mrs. Neville, in answer to Mr. Golding.

The Church was not with Mr. Benison the be-all and end-all; there was something better—even the people who went there, and the people who stayed away. Mr. Benison made no pretensions to carry St. Peter's keys on the same ring with those that opened his desk or his sideboard. He had never read a word of Hegel or Strauss, and therefore, unlike many estimable divines, did not endeavour to confute them. Neither did he attempt to trace his own genealogical pedigree up

to the apostles, and does not think it necessary
to refer to a spiritual herald's office to determine
his apostolical succession. But there is still one
opinion of his, which, I fear, may shock many of
his brethren. He was an anti-sabbatarian, as it
is called, that is to say, he did not wish to con-
fine people to mere Sabbath day's journeys. He
was even a promoter of Sunday cheap excursion-
trains, which should carry the mechanics of Stoke
Furnace beyond the monotonous clank of engines,
and the scorching blast-fires, which shrivel the
skin and calcine the very bones, into green wood-
lands and meadow-lands. But how came Mr.
Benison with these ideas? The answer is easy.
Mr. Benison was himself one of the people, the
son of a small, struggling manufacturer, who had
originally been a mechanic, and had known the
hardships of the poor. Mr. Benison had known
what it is to be suffocated in flues of streets,
where the smoke curls along as up a chimney,
and where the soot-flakes dye the linen hung on
the line; had endured, too, the stench-pools which
never ebb, had gasped for breath in hot dungeons

called rooms. Oh, my dear possessor of parks,
and picture-galleries, and gardens, be not so indignant with Mr. Benison, but think with pity
on the poor prisoners of Stoke Furnace, toiling
night and day in sweat and dirt; think of their
little, crippled, pale-faced children, and grudge
them not their scanty Sabbath's enjoyment.

" We shall drive you home," said Mrs. Neville
to Mr. Golding at luncheon.

Their road was to Stoke Furnace, where he
wanted to stop, and where his own carriage
would meet him. Stoke Furnace lies in a vale,
and seems ever to be one of those cities destroyed
by fire, such a continual smoke and flame rise
up from it. You may tell when you are approaching this city of volcanoes by the black
leaves on the posts, for they cannot be called
trees. In the distance tower high black chimneys, from which issue solid columns of smoke,
so solid and thick that you know not where the
chimney ends and the smoke begins. And then
you fancy that you see steaming geysers and
lava-pools, but these are only engines steaming

and burning slag, and "hovels" where the earthenware is burnt; and then as night draws on, you see one by one the furnace fires burn out brilliantly, casting their yellow tawny floods of light across the road, and the flames brandishing themselves from the chimney mouths, like fiery swords leaping from dark scabbards, piercing the darkness. But by day it is all darkness, all black; a land colonized by the descendants of Ham. The streets of Stoke Furnace are built apparently as irregularly as human ingenuity can devise. Each squatter had built himself a "hovel" where he thought most fit. Very sharp curves, and immense troops of black children there are, as Reginald finds out, who is on the box-seat driving. Rails are laid down in the streets, but they are of exactly the same colour as the black road, so that you do not see them at first. Swing-bridges cross canals apparently full of ink, where float barges like great dark hearses. Railways run along their sides, where slow, heavily laden, groaning trains crawl like long black caterpillars, throwing up their black streams of smoke, which quickly mix in the great pall that broods over the city. Little yellow dismal jets shine in the street lamps, though it is a fine summer after- noon. A sort of debateable land is this between the potteries and the real iron districts. You know not where they join; this seems to belong to neither, but both—the Berwick-upon-Sewer of Ironshire. Here they are at Mr. Golding's offices.

"Come along to us, Reginald, and let the coachman drive home," cries Minnie, when old Mr. Golding has left.

So he gladly comes and sits by Minnie, who has made room for him. Mrs. Neville is lean- ing out of the carriage sorrowfully looking at all the wretchedness as they drive through the back lanes: but all the streets of Stoke Furnace are the same; so it is ridiculous to call any of them more especially back or front. There goes Mr. Benison toiling along. He has not had a mo- ment's rest since he left. He is far too intent upon his work to see them. A great ball of dust is rolling up the street, and breaks upon

him like grape-shot. But on he hurries. Dust
and heat, wet and frost, cannot easily interfere
with such a man. And now he is out of sight.
The carriage crosses the canal, that black Styx
which separates the nether regions of Stoke
Furnace from the light and gladness of the world
of sunshine. Gradually the road becomes less
black; gradually the leaves seem really to flutter,
and not look like iron imitations; gradually the
voices of birds steal on you, and you find yourself at last in the country, with Bushwood before
you.

A new schoolroom was begun with Mr. Golding's aid, and went on famously. Mr. Aston
Neville came down at last, and talked a great
deal about Government education and Government grants, but somehow or another, when, at
Mrs. Neville's request, Reginald wrote to the
Government authorities for assistance, they found
out that their school had a stone, and Government
required a wooden, floor, or exactly the reverse;
that Government required a roof a certain shape;
in fact, Government seemed to invent the most

ingenious excuses why it should not grant money
to Bushwood school.

"I think some day we shall have a letter from
Government commanding us to pull down the
whole building," said Mrs. Neville, after reading
one of the Government printed forms.

Parliament was not yet dissolved, so Mr.
Aston Neville was only down occasionally, and
all the Bushwood cricket and archery parties
were always fixed for those times when he would
be at home. Lord Cokeborough was, as usual,
often over at Bushwood, and paid greater attention than formerly to Miss Minnie.

"There is Lord Cokeborough with Minnie,"
Mrs. Neville would jokingly say to Reginald,
which made him think that she knew more about
Minnie and himself than he formerly fancied.
But he noticed this also, that she would often
steal away from all the great parties to her poor
children.

During one of these archery meetings Reginald
once went away with her; their path lay through
the woods. Little breezes wandered up and down

30—2

the paths and avenues, as if they had lost their way, and could never again escape. The dove was sleepily cooing in the firs. The white butter-fly-orchis flung out its sweetest perfumes. Their path went by the old church of St. John's in the Wilderness, as it was called, the same church that Reginald's father had gone to to see the monuments to his own father and mother. Deserted it had been for some years, and for that same period had its tithes been appropriated by Mr. Aston Neville. The whole of the church though was still standing, but in so unsafe a condition that service was never performed. A long, low wall with a stile in the centre, fenced in the graveyard from the wood, but the flowers had clambered over the wall, for there were as many in the churchyard as in the wood.

"Come, let us sit down upon the stile, and rest, for I am tired," said Mrs. Neville, and of late she had suffered a good deal from over-work at the school. The old graveyard had been long neglected. Rank grass grew luxuriantly in those grave furrows, which separate grave from grave.

Lichens now gilded the few words on each humble
stone. Tall nettles stood like sentinels beside each
green mound, from amongst which the white-
throat flew out with its sweet wild song. Some old
yews bent over the church-door, making a natural
porch; and skirting the graveyard on the farther
side runs a pure brook separating with its crystal
barrier this sombre place from the rest of the world·

"I know not why I like this old churchyard
so much," said Mrs. Neville, "for not one person
buried here did I ever know," she continued, pen-
sively. "Come, let us go, and peep in at the windows;" and they looked through the greenish gray
glass, and could see the Bible still open on the
reading-desk, and the prayer-books in some of the
pews; everything still the same as on that Sunday, when a large piece of the roof tumbled down
in the middle of service, and frightened out the
congregation. No one had since entered. The
old walls had sunk; their stone knees were bent.
The setting sun now streamed through the west
painted window, turning the common pavement,
and the white plastered walls, into marble, rich

with a thousand colours. A robin was perched in the aisle and sang his anthem unto God. The old place was not deserted. Worshippers has God, though no congregation of men and women ever knelt to Him.

Up at the schoolroom they found Mr. Benison very busy; in fact, he spared a portion of nearly every day to come over. The new schoolroom, too, was fast progressing, the window-sills were now fixed, and looked like great sockets wanting their eyes.

Mrs. Neville, in her quiet, unassuming way, superintended everything. How quiet is everything that is productive of good! How quietly the gentle rain falls, turning itself hour by hour into sweetest flowers! how gently does the green shoot spring from the ground! how quietly does the bud form itself! how softly the flower expands! until unexpectedly it blooms before you, clothed in beauty and light. So quiet and gentle was Lucy Neville in all her acts: no noise, no self-praise, but that simple quiet modesty which so enhances every deed.

CHAPTER XII.

A NARROW ESCAPE.

THE heavy school-work soon began to tell on Mrs. Neville, and she must evidently have some relaxation. Little Flo, too, who was by no means strong, felt the hot weather, and the doctor ordered his two patients to the sea-side. Where to go was the next consideration. Mr. Aston Neville proposed some fashionable watering-place, but this was negatived by Miss Minnie, who declared,—

"There is no enjoyment under the shadow of fashion. Supposing we go to Limpetstone or Aqua Marina, it is but Belgravia and bathing-machines. I know every shell and stone on the beach at Aqua Marina; the sea-weed at Aqua Marina is more like wet black hay than genuine sea-weed. At Aqua Marina the tide comes in as slowly, as if the great sea were a flunkey, and afraid to wet all the fashionable Canutes."

So spoke Miss Minnie on the subject. Mr. Aston Neville, however, had a double object in choosing Aqua Marina. It was near London, and he could easily run down; and secondly, Lord Cokeborough was just now stopping there; but somehow or another, Mr. Aston Neville was over-ruled. Miss Minnie was very nearly telling him that he knew Lord Cokeborough was at Aqua Marina, and that was his reason for wish-ing to go there; but a look from her mother checked this speech.

"Ah!" said Mrs. Neville to Reginald after one of these Aqua Marina debates. "Aston will willingly pay ten guineas a-week as long as we like at Aqua Marina, but grudges a mite for the school; really it is too hard!" and it was too hard, considering that so much of Mr. Aston Neville's property came from her. "And for this reason," she added, "I should like to go to some quiet place, if was merely to save the money." So, after much looking in various maps, they fixed upon the town of Pen-in-y-ynk in North Wales. They chose it because some fashionable guide book had characterised it " as very wild," and deemed it quite beneath its dignity to say anything more. So Mrs. Neville made a bargain with her husband, that she was to have so much money wherever they went, and the cousins agreed among themselves, that they would be as economical as possible, and save what they could for the school.

How to reach Pen-in-y-ynk was the difficulty. Railroads stopped suddenly short, whenever they went in the direction of Pen-in-y-ynk. The map all round Pen-in-y-ynk was shaded with the thickest ink, indicating high mountains, and consequently not many turnpike roads. As Mr. Aston Neville was not going, he did not trouble himself about the matter, but returned to London. Mrs. Neville went to take a long look at the school before they started, and begged Mr. Benison to write and give an account of how things went on. The carriage had taken them to the

Stoke Furnace station. The footman stared when Reginald ordered him to place all the cloaks and shawls in a second-class carriage. Alfred Craven, who happened to be on the platform, stared too with his eyeglass at the proceeding, and wonders whether they have all gone mad, or suddenly run short of money.

"We are going to see the world, Mr. Craven, and shall begin our observations from a second-class carriage," said Minnie to him. "Come, I know you are going down the line, and so had better jump in with us," she continued.

Alfred Craven looks round him, and when he thinks no one sees him, jumps in, in the most melancholy fashion. They have the carriage all to themselves. Alfred Craven stops at the next station, and is sadly mortified at being detected by certain friends stepping out from a second-class.

"Did you notice," said Minnie, "how all the railway porters stared at us at Ironton?"

Reginald had not then had much leisure to

watch their countenances, for as they took no servants, he had the care of the luggage, and was studying arithmetic from Mr. Bradshaw's amusing guide.

"Put away that book, Regy," said Minnie, taking it from him.

"I think we are quite as comfortable in here as we should have been in a first-class," said Mrs. Neville.

"I am sure we are quite as happy," added Minnie, and she was determined she would be.

They bought newspapers at stations, they laughed and joked, for they had still the carriage to themselves. Presently in came a butcher with a greasy blue smockfrock. My polite reader, do not be shocked. He came and sat next to Miss Minnie. Do not, I pray, pity Minnie; pity rather the poor butcher, for that young lady, with great presence of mind, instantly handed him Bradshaw, and begged of him in the most winning manner to find out the way to Pen-in-y-ynk, North Wales. The poor butcher set to work in a thorough John Bull style. He scratched his head; he greased the book all over; but Bradshaw beat him.

" After all that hard work, I am sure you will want some refreshment," said Minnie, opening a packet of sandwiches, and handing them to the butcher still puzzling over Bradshaw, for he did not like to confess he was beaten.

" Drat such a book as this, it is of no good, nohow," said he, red in the face with excitement; and it was with difficulty Reginald prevented him from flinging Bradshaw out of the window. He left them very soon, with an injunction to Minnie, that whatever she did, "don't you use such a book as that; it ain't no good to nobody."

However, by its help, and that of sundry intelligent porters, they arrived exactly too late for the steamer at Liverpool, for North Wales.

The next day was still fine, and in the morning they started.

"Now, Nep, don't jump overboard in your excitement in beholding the sea," said Minnie to old Nep, whom they had brought, and who had travelled in grand state in a cattle van, for none of the railway dog-kennels would hold him, and Nep's feelings on board the steamer were apparently very similar to those of the soldiers in Xenophon, when they again beheld the sea. All was bright and sunny. The steamer seemed to be supported on the water by merely its paddle-wheels. The calm sunshine lay upon the calm water, as though you might have taken them both up together. In the distance, flocks of vessels spread out their white wings waiting to catch the breeze. The dim outline of a coast, the hazy Welsh mountains, now faintly heave in sight. The island of Anglesea, the Great Orme's Head, the Menai Straits, one by one present themselves as in some dreamy vision, and then the two bridges, one woven as with threads of gossamer, the other huge and heavy, yet full of grandeur and Titan-like majesty. Past Beau-maris, and up the straits, and a little boat takes

them off to Bangor, where they pass the
night.

The next day they are travelling amongst the
Welsh mountains, in quest of Pen-in-y-ynk.
They arrive there late at night, after much
trouble in procuring horses at the roadside inns.
They once went part of the road drawn by a team
of cart-horses, exactly as if they had been a plough,
as Minnie remarked. No hotel had Pen-in-y-ynk,
but a primitive inn, far better than any hotel.
The next day they found lodgings at an English
settler's, who had established himself in the double
occupation of farmer and fisherman, an amphi-
bious sort of being, whose wife was general inter-
preter between them and the natives.

Pen-in-y-ynk stands in a sort of cleft of the
mountains, wedged so tightly in, that it cannot be shaken by the wildest storms. Great
high mountains, nearly barren, towered on all
sides, the sea ever tumbling and foaming, so
different to the still blue pool at Aqua Marina,
whilst long strips of sand stretched away for miles,
so fine, that you might imagine the contents of

all the hour-glasses in England had been emptied
here. The tide here seemed never to run out,
always full, always foaming and splashing; and
the waves were ever running races, just like little
blue-eyed children bounding away from their
mother-ocean up to a certain mark on the beach,
which they just touched, and then hurried back
to her arms again.

The first day that they walked on the sands
it seemed as if the ocean had been gathering
during the summer its harvest of sea-weed.
Great sheaves of it lay on the shore. Here it
crackled under their feet, there it covered the
rocks with its fine green moss. Along the sands
used these four to walk : all day long were they
down on them, and took everything with them—
books, letters, luncheon, dinner, tea. A colour
was blooming in the pale cheeks of little Flo,
and Mrs. Neville soon felt stronger; and as for
Minnie, she was more handsome than ever.
Long, long strolls did Minnie and Reginald take
by themselves, Minnie singing her songs from
the *Tempest*, and looking herself divine as some

fairy Ariel. Hand in hand did they walk by the great sea, listening to its grand poetry, and the musical rhythmic measure of its waves. Venus, they say, rose out of the sea, and a fine old parable it is, for by the sea the heart always seems to open wider, and divine impulses and divine yearnings, coming we know not whence, thrill through us. Many and many were the reveries of love those two dreamed.

To-day they were sitting by themselves on the sands close to a margin of pebbles, which the waves rolled together with a trailing sound, polishing them, as it were, and then arranging them again, as though not quite pleased.

"Of course you know, Regy, that mamma is aware of our engagement," said Minnie, breaking away from one of these day-dreams.

"I thought you promised not to tell her," Reginald replied, "at least, just at present."

"But she knew it as soon as I did," was the answer; "and there was no concealing it from her; besides, she is so well pleased."

Reginald's face flushed a little when he returned to Mrs. Neville. Little Flo was some way off amusing herself with sending Nep on various commissions into the water.

"Why, you silly Reginald, do you suppose I was so blind as not to perceive your love?" replied Mrs. Neville, in answer to an allusion of his. "Do you suppose you would ever have been allowed to have stayed at Bushwood if I had not screened you in a thousand ways from Aston? Come here and sit by my side, you two." And Mrs. Neville opened her inmost heart to them. She told them how wretched she felt through her husband's meanness and love of money and rank, that she had made up her mind that Minnie should never marry Lord Cokeborough; and she continued,—"I have ever loved you as a son, Reginald; I have loved you because I saw a nobleness in your disposition, which hated injustice and tyranny, and which despised mere wealth."

Reginald looked up and saw Mrs. Neville's eyes filled with tears. He kissed them away, for he dearly loved her. She had, as she said, treated him as a son; had been a true mother to the orphan. They all of them felt happier. There was a smile upon Mrs. Neville's face when she saw Minnie and Reginald together; they were her own daughter and son, and proud was Reginald to have such a mother; but they would have a long time to wait. How Mr. Aston Neville's consent was to be obtained they knew not. Much was still left to be solved by the future.

But they had been staying here too long talking; the tide had risen quite unperceived: they had been sitting in a small bay formed like a half-moon, whose two ends were locked by high rocks against which the sea was now running. A breeze, too, was freshening up, and the full moon, which now rose slowly, told Reginald it would be a higher tide than usual. The long waves came rolling in, now one, and then two at a time, sometimes in confusion jostling against one another, and sometimes breaking far out at sea, as if they had mistaken their time. Nothing all round but the great ocean, which now began to renew its daily battle against its passive but firm enemy, the land, which frowned down in contempt; and now here and there the beach was strewn with bits of spars, which the waves kept throwing up into a sort of spoil-bank, sad trophies of their victories, and the white masses of foam began to drift along the shore. Reginald saw that the only chance of escape was now; for in another five minutes all retreat would be cut off. He hurried his cousins to the west corner as fast as he could: already the waves were beating up the rocks, climbing up the steepest places wherever they could find a cranny to catch hold or a ledge to support themselves, and then exhausted, falling back, leaving the sands bare. The only chance was to take advantage of the retiring wave and so get round the corner. But this required great judgment and nicety, as every now and then the wind would bring a wave faster and higher than usual.

"Stay here," cried Reginald to Mrs. Neville and Minnie, who were now awake to their danger, placing them on a table-rock above the waves; "don't move till I come—" and snatching up little

Flo in his arms he carried her to the base of the rocks.

At that moment a heavy sea broke, covering him with spray. Mrs. Neville shrieked, thinking he was washed off, but he merely waved his hand, and the instant the water began to retire he rushed through it. In a moment he was across, and little Flo safely landed. Watching his opportunity he was soon back to his cousins. Minnie he safely carried over in the same manner; but Mrs. Neville said she would rather cross by herself. Reginald tried to dissuade her, but in vain. She stood for a time with her eyes fixed upon the waves, still hesitating.

"Now is the time!" cried Reginald, as the waters left the sands bare; but she stopped, then started. "It is too late now!" shouted Reginald, but she heard him not.

Reginald rushed after her—grasped her hand. She turned to look: behind she saw the great wave close at her heels.

"Run for your life!" cried Reginald, endeavouring to pull her along, but she was rooted to the spot. He seized her tightly round the waist, and planted his foot firm against the sand, determined if possible to stand the shock. Up came the wave, breaking with all its fury over him, knocking him to the ground; but he did not loose his hold. For a moment all was calm; he had time to prepare himself for the backwater which came with baffled fury from the rocks: once more he was knocked down, but still clung to his burden. The water rushed over him, dragging him to the sea: within two yards of it was he, when once more springing to his feet he seized Mrs. Neville, and made with her to the shore. The wave rushed after him white with rage and maddened at having let go its prey from its clutch; it was a race for life; close to his heels did it break, but its violence was now spent, and he safely reached the high shingle.

The people from the village, alarmed at their absence, had come down to the shore. They carried poor Mrs. Neville, half dead with fear and exhaustion, in their arms up the cliff. She was quickly put to bed, and Minnie became her nurse. There was not one of the cousins that night who did not think of the scene which took place at Morley many years ago, and how near it was being repeated that very day.

CHAPTER XIII.

THE VALLEY OF THE SHADOW OF DEATH.

THE long vacation was past. Reginald was once more in Oxford reading hard with Amherst. No boating, no cricketing this term. He knew that all his prospects depended on his own exertions; and this, and the feeling of duty and love, gave him a strong impetus to work. Late at night in one another's rooms did they sit making analyses and notes, oftentimes into the morning when the stars were shining bright into the dim quad.

From Bushwood he used to hear very frequently. "Poor mamma is very unwell," writes Minnie to-day; and a letter the next morning and the following bring worse news. It is the end of term. Reginald hurries off to Bushwood. He meets Minnie in the entrance hall, looking very pale and ill.

"Dear mamma is no better, I fear," said the poor girl, with tears in her eyes.

At this moment Dr. Hester came down the stairs and entered the library. Poor Mrs. Neville was dangerously ill with a low fever, brought on partly by the shock she had sustained on the sea-shore, and over-work at the school. The doctor would not leave the house.

"The crisis of the disease will be to-night. Has Mr. Neville been sent for? if not, he must be telegraphed for immediately," he said.

Minnie came crying into the room.

"Oh, Reginald, I am perfectly miserable; here is papa away——"

The kind doctor stopped her. She came and leant her burning face against Reginald's bosom. The darkness keeps increasing. The fire flings out great gaunt shadows like those of Death itself, which flicker and hover about, as if they would seize their prey. The doctor had left the room. You would not know there was any one in it, but by Minnie's sobs. If they would see Mrs. Neville alive once more, they must go now. Poor Minnie can scarcely drag herself up the stairs. They enter the room. A dim light is burning; and you can see a little child kneeling by the bedside and offering up its prayers to spare mamma: it is little Flo. Poor Minnie goes to the bedside, and in utter despair buries her head in the bed-clothes; Mrs. Neville is asleep, but now awakens. She stretches a white thin hand from under the coverlet to reach Reginald, but is too weak. She looks towards Minnie. The poor girl started, and stretched her hand to her dying mother, who took it with Reginald's.

Mrs. Neville tried to speak, and they could hear her faintly say,—

"I give her to you, Regy; love her and little Flo for my sake, and God bless you, darlings."

The effort was too much; she turned on her side, and only moved once or twice when the door opened, as if looking for her husband. They knew not when she was dead.

"It is all over," whispered the doctor.

"Oh! I won't believe it," cried Minnie in an agony of despair; and she fell senseless beside the bed, and was carried out of the room.

Poor little Flo was still kneeling beside the bed repeating her prayers, and thinking that mamma was only asleep, and they carried her away, too, in their arms. And there lay Lucy Neville, calm and quiet, with a sweet sad smile on her countenance, as if grief and love still contended for the mastery,—love for her children, grief for her wretched husband. Reginald now felt twice an orphan.

In the morning Mr. Aston Neville came. Reginald met the miserable man in the front doorway. He knew not how to treat him. Contempt was uppermost in his mind.

" No; she died not so much from fever, as from your coldness," he answered, when Aston Neville spoke of his wife's death, for Reginald was pained at his thorough heartlessness.

Mr. Aston Neville excused himself on the plea of important business.

" We will see to the funeral, then, if you would like to return; there is a train starts immediately;"

for Reginald did not care to conceal his feelings.

At this moment Minnie entered the room, looking so pale and haggard that her father scarcely knew her. She came to Reginald, and took his hand, the tears still breaking in a storm from her eyes.

Aston again excused himself for coming too late.

" Yes, I can readily believe you would have felt some pleasure in witnessing the death of one whom you always treated so shamefully in her lifetime," Reginald replied, in bitter tones.

" You shall leave the house, sir; come away from him, Minnie," Aston weakly said; but Minnie only held Reginald's hand faster than before.

" When I quit this house, your daughter quits it with me," Reginald replied. " She is the legacy your wife left me last night—the only legacy she had the power to leave; for I believe you have long ago taken care of everything else she once possessed."

Aston came up to take his daughter from him. Reginald would have felled him to the ground; but Minnie clung round him crying— begging him not to touch her father.

"I have spared you for the sake of your daughter. Do not drive her also to the grave," said Reginald, as he thrust him aside.

A week of mourning, a week of tears and of sobs did the cousins spend. Reginald could not bear to see Aston, and lived upstairs with Minnie and Flo. A memorandum had been found in Mrs. Neville's desk, begging that she might be buried quietly in one corner of the old Bush- wood churchyard. Then came that second death, that bitterest separation of all. As long as they had her in the house, she still seemed one of them. They could go to her lying in the coffin, and kiss her; ay, poor little Flo would still say her prayers by the coffin side, and beg God in such accents—that God himself could not help listening—to take care of her mamma. But they were now coming to carry her away. As long as the cousins could see her face she still seemed theirs; but now they would nail down the lid, and they should never more see her. The workmen were waiting outside the room, but the cousins would not leave. Minnie hung over her mother's face. They had placed what few winter flowers they could find in the coffin with her. One long, long—last kiss.

"Oh! do not nail mamma up," cried little Flo in childish agony; but as they sat weeping together in another room, they could hear the nails driven in.

It was bitterly cold on the day of Mrs. Neville's funeral. Their way to the old churchyard lay through the woods where they had so often been all together. The trees which, when they last walked there, were green with leaves, and their bark covered with a gold frieze of moss, looked now mere bare iron posts with patches of rust. A dim, leaden-coloured sky was overhead, the wind blowing keenly, and roaring fitfully in blasts in the deep woods. Mr. Benison read the service, and when those solemn words, "dust to dust, ashes to ashes," were pronounced, and when the clod broke heavily upon the coffin-lid, and the red worm crawled out, Minnie fell forward, almost into her mother's grave.

" I cannot bear to see it," she cried. Reginald sprang to her, " Save me, Regy," and she sank into his arms.

Poor Mrs. Neville had but little to leave; and yet who ever left so much ? The money bequeathed us is spent in a few years more or less; but a legacy of love and kindness is treasured up for ever. All Mrs. Neville's property had been assigned over to Aston by her marriage settlement. Since then she had received a small sum from an aunt, which she left in equal shares to Minnie and Flo, under the trusteeship of old Mr. Golding, who was now a real and true friend. Each day showed in him little touching traits of kindness, which only a feeling heart can suggest. Minnie and Reginald revealed to him the true state of matters.

" As to the schools, Minnie, I will find the funds to maintain them. Do not fear. But in this matter of yours and Reginald's, I know not what to say."

Minnie told him her mother's dying words.

"I know it all quite well; she often mentioned it to me," said the old man, sadly. "You must both of you wait, and then see if your father, Minnie, will approve of the marriage:" for old Mr. Golding knew very well that in the present state of things Aston's consent could never be obtained. Mr. Aston Neville had already wedded Minnie in his imagination to a coronet. He had bought a niche in Debrets' gallery for his daughter. He might himself actually become the grandfather of a host of little coronets. "And," continued Mr. Golding, "your cousin Reginald will, I trust, distinguish himself at Oxford, and your father —"

"Whatever Regy does at Oxford, he will ever be mine," said Minnie.

"But one thing," continued Mr. Golding, "seems imperative, that Reginald should not any longer stay here. You will certainly not achieve your ends by your present method."

They both saw the soundness of his advice, for from the day of poor Mrs. Neville's death, Aston and Reginald had not spoken even a friendly word, or even sat together in the same room.

"You are still very young, Minnie, and you can contrive to wait till Reginald has taken his degree, and settled down to some profession," said Mr. Golding.

"I will wait for ever for him, if it be necessary," cried Minnie.

"I hope to be able to earn my own living at the bar in a few years," said Reginald, for he repudiated the idea of living upon poor Minnie's scanty pittance, which he knew would be all she would certainly ever possess if she married him against her father's consent.

Mr. Aston Neville in the meanwhile had written to Colonel Ancaster, and told him it was far from convenient to keep Reginald, and that as he was still under age the colonel was his legal guardian. Reginald soon received a letter from the colonel on the subject, commanding him

to report himself, as the colonel's phrase ran, at
Merepool early next week.

Poor Minnie was strangely altered by her
mother's death. It was the first real grief the
poor girl had ever known, and she consequently
felt it far more than those who meet with daily
struggles in a world of poverty. Yet there are
some whom black mourning shows to better advantage than a ball-room dress. So was it with
Minnie. Her liveliness and mirth had forsaken
her, but in their place were all the more con-
spicuously seen her tender-heartedness and love.
Only the winter reveals to us in the bare hedges
all the warm nestling places which the birds
have built, and such warm nestling places were
there in Minnie's breast.

Poor little Flo's grief for her mother seemed
never to be staunched. She was far more delicate and weak than Minnie, and the shock had
taken a great effect upon her. Besides, she could
not, like Minnie, relieve her sorrow by working
in the school. In this way, by doing what she
thought her mother would most have approved,

did Minnie extinguish much of the flame of grief,
which burnt itself into poor little Flo's heart.
Mr. Aston Neville bore his grief so well that
you might have imagined he was the best Christian that ever breathed.

But the time was approaching when Reginald
must leave. Minnie and he went to all the old
haunts where Mrs. Neville had so often been
with them. Everything seemed to mourn her—
the dead branches, the silent birds, the mute
streams. They went—little Flo was with them—
to her grave, and there those three stood in silent
sorrow. They could have knelt down and kissed
the grass which covered her grave. One snow-
drop was just peeping above it, the only one in
the old churchyard, so white, so pure, like an
angel guarding that tomb.

Then came their own parting. Mrs. Neville's
dying words they repeated to one another, and so
with kisses and tears they parted.

CHAPTER XIV.

MEREPOOL ABBEY AGAIN.

THREE years had passed since Reginald was at Merepool. There was still the same old conservative look about the place. The old trees still blossomed with the same notices they had done for years before. Up the long avenue Reginald slowly walked. The carriage was at the door, and his aunt and cousins were just going out for a drive. They did not know him again until he introduced himself to them. Nor did they know him then, he thought. Lady Mary held out a glove to him, in which he supposed there was a hand; and his cousins Charlotte and Elizabeth held out to him various coloured gloves, in which he supposed there were also hands, with fingers and a pulse; but he would never have been able to have discovered this by their method of shaking hands.

Napoleon said of the Bourbons, they never learnt anything or ever forgot anything. And this was precisely the case with the Ancasters. You gathered the same notions of the Ancasters from their conversation that you might have done any number of years ago—that the Ancasters were the *Dii Indigenæ* of the fens, the Αὐτόχθονες of Fentonshire, that Fentonshire was never without them and the grasshoppers; and without them, not only Fentonshire, but all England would be speedily ruined. This last was always the climax of all the colonel's speeches. England was certainly, even according to him, a long time in being ruined, for it was nearly thirty years since he first made.the prophecy.

Gravestone and Surplyce lived still at their respective quarters. The same old people, with the same old notions, still came to the Merepool dinner-parties—the old Duke of Fentonshire, and his son the Marquis of Fenton, and old Mr. John Horney of Horney; and they talked their old nonsense,

which they had talked all their lives, and would
continue to talk if their lives lasted a thousand
years. In fact, Merepool Abbey seemed to have
had one long sleep since Reginald was away, and
its inmates were only now waking up, and finish-
ing the tasks which they just began when he left.
Her ladyship was still busy working at a curious
breed of dogs, which are seen only in German
worsted-work. It was the same breed, the same
dog, she was busy at three years ago. The
colonel was engaged at precisely the same old
work of drawing up warrants for the committal
of poachers, for precisely the same old offences.
Charlotte Ancaster, on the same conservative principles, was not yet married to the gallant Saber,
who was still staying at Merepool, and who looked
as if he had not yet thoroughly awoke from his
three years' nap. His moustache still slept.

"Whom are you in mourning for?" one day
asked Charlotte.

Reginald replied, for his cousin.

"I suppose you don't wish us to go into mourning also?" she answered, with a sneer.

"You are not even good enough to mourn for one who was so pure," thought Reginald to himself, but restrained himself from saying so. At this moment the colonel entered the room, and the conversation turned from poor Mrs. Neville's death, to manufacturers, and the manufacturing classes, and the great danger ensuing from such people.

"It strikes me, Colonel Ancaster, that you are extremely ignorant of the manufacturing classes," said Reginald, for the colonel had still all the Fentonshire country gentleman's fears about the manufacturers and the chartists, which he supposed to be synonymous, and was for applying the remedy of the sword or the bayonet to cut or disentangle every social difficulty. And so uncle and nephew were still not on the best of terms. The colonel disliked Mr. Aston Neville's politics, and thought Reginald must have embraced them. He little knew how Reginald hated them. Still stern, yet in his heart kind, still proud yet able, ever taking for granted that he was in the right, and every one else in the wrong, he was still the same

Colonel Ancaster. Years had brought him no
lesson. Experience left no teaching on him.

Reginald had plenty to occupy him, for he was
now reading hard. He felt himself quite independent of his cousins. He knew well the meaning
of the Roman emperor's saying, " *Nunquam mi-
nus solus quam cum solus.*" Up in his room in
the tower would he study through the winter
days, watching the silent snow fall over the wide
fen-lands, like seed cast abroad, by the hand of
God high up in heaven.

Then there was also the library at the top of
the abbey, where Reginald had before scarcely
ever been, but where he now found great delight
in his leisure hours. No one ever went there
but himself. A fine high room it was, lighted
by dormer windows, its walls lined with panels
painted over with flowers and various devices,
under which you might, if you looked very
closely, just discern the features of some of the old
cavaliers peeping forth. Under thick layers and
deposits of dust did the books lie cropping out
here and there in irregular strata. They were

the fossil remains of a long past literary age, types of broadsheets, and little dumpy volumes, looking like nodules, that now no longer exist. Then there were, too, a great many specimens of those primitive and simpler forms of literary life, generally called manuscript. Most of these were written during the early and middle part of the seventeenth century, and referred to the great controversies then raging. At first they were a great puzzle and contradiction, written in one's own language, and yet not written in one's own handwriting or spelling; and Reginald found he had not so much to learn as to unlearn, in fact, to forget the A B C of childhood, and make a fresh alphabet of the mother tongue. Many a happy leisure hour would he spend, deciphering these old manuscripts.

Long letters, too, came from Minnie, who now wrote in better spirits. But little Flo is not so well. Kind old Mr. Golding has asked them both to pay a visit as long as they like to him. The schools, too, are progressing, thanks to that good old man.

" And when do you propose taking your degree ? " asked the colonel.

" Somewhere about this time next year," Reginald replied.

" I have made arrangements with Mr. Gravestone to take you as his curate here."

Reginald thanked the colonel, but added he had not the slightest intention of entering the church.

" And good God, sir, what course do you intend to pursue ? "

Reginald replied, that he thought he should enter at the bar, if his degree were high enough to warrant such a course.

" As you please, sir, as you please ; but I should like to know where you are going to procure the funds for such a profession. Are you at all aware what your balance is at my banker's ? "

Reginald was, in fact, totally ignorant, and told him so.

" It is now only somewhere about five hundred pounds, and, by God, sir, I should like to

know how you intend to keep yourself as a gentleman, and eat your terms with that sum ! "

Reginald told him that whatever he did, he
should certainly not enter the church.

" And what, sir, may be your reason ? "

" If there was no other objection, I should
certainly never agree to becoming Mr. Gravestone's curate."

" And what have you to say against Mr.
Gravestone ? " he continued, rather wóndering,
for Gravestone was the colonel's model clergyman.

" I will only mention one, and that, perhaps,
the very least; Mr. Gravestone, as you know
well, is nothing else but your private chaplain,
and I will never consent to enter the pulpit as
his assistant."

The colonel's anger was great: but anger is
not the best possible argument. He wished to
know the other reasons. Reginald, with a little
asperity, told him they were such, as from their
nature, he could never be brought to understand.

" Do you think, then, that the church is an

ungentlemanly profession?" the colonel asked, after a long pause, as though after much puzzling he had hit upon the only tenable objection. Reginald could not help smiling. "Why, sir, I am going to make my youngest son a clergyman; and if it is good enough for him, it ought to be for you," he continued.

"It is partly this, Colonel Ancaster, that makes the church what it is; people like yourself thrusting younger sons into it. Estates and money are entailed upon the eldest, but the church is now the estate and money entailed upon the younger sons of good families."

The colonel was hurt. He meant well. He had no other idea but that of benefiting his nephew and placing him in a good position in society; and he thought, as many estimable people still think, that Providence has given the Established Church of England, with that special object in view, to the younger sons or the poor relations of good families. The colonel, however, imagined, that when the time came, Reginald's objections would vanish, that the shortness of his purse would weigh strongly with him, and said as much—

" By God, sir, if you like to starve you can; but remember I have done my part in the matter."

And so the colonel had.

CHAPTER XV.

EXPULSION FROM OXFORD.

REGINALD was now in his third year at college.
He had long since left Pogis's and Slowcombe's
lectures, and gone into those of Lowndes and
Cayley, the subrector, who wrote the beautiful
Latin prose. When Cayley lectured on the
Articles, he always seemed to be thinking whether
they would turn into good Ciceronian Latin.
Cayley, it was said, could never read the Latin
Fathers; they wrote so ungrammatically. But it
was Lowndes who really influenced Reginald's
mind, and exercised, as a tutor should ever do,
not only his pupil's intellectual, but his moral
qualities. Reginald and Amherst had, too, in
private worked hard together, and there was every
chance of their both taking " firsts."

It was now the October term, and in the spring Reginald would take his degree. He had also put on a "coach," and used to go to his rooms in the evening to read. The fifth of November, with its civil war, was now coming upon Oxford, and arousing the martial feelings of its inhabitants. This year, various incidents proved that the annual fight would be on a grand scale. The senior proctor this year belonged to the peace-party, and had issued a bulletin that any under-graduate engaged in the riot, would suffer various penalties, thus giving a most unfair advantage to the "town," and the enemy gained great confidence in consequence. Reginald had quite forgotten the whole affair, as he was returning in the evening from his "coach's" rooms. On he walked, baited the whole way by a pack of small boys shouting "gown" at him.

"Go away," said Reginald; but they still kept snapping and yelping "gown" at him.

The scene soon changed as he turned into the main streets. The proctor's orders had been most ineffectual. Skirmishes were going on all

over Oxford. St. Matthew's college, with its old
gray walls, looked now like some grim fortress.
The porter's lodge was turned into a keep, from
whence bands of men poured forth, carrying
everything before them: whilst a party of men,
like amateur engineers, had fortified the battle-
ments of St. Mark's, and were playfully assaulting
the mob below with lumps of coal, which the
mob retaliated by breaking St. Mark's windows.
A troop of light skirmishers from Jericho dashed
down Ethelred's lane, with their war-cry of
" Town !" to the rescue, but the well-directed black
artillery swept the street.

And now began the fight. " Gown!" " gown!"
" Town !" " town!" fiercely sounded in every-
direction, as the mob was murdering a small de-
tachment of men separated from the main troop.
Reginald could not idly pass by and see this;
he rushed to the rescue, his papers and notes
flying to the wind. In a moment he was in the
thickest of the fight, and his English blood was
up. It was three to one; but the " gown " cared
not. Reginald put his back to the street-wall,

and hit out in desperation. The little band formed together, and under Reginald's direction charged upon the mob. "Neville of St. Matthew's," was a name known throughout Oxford in those days ; and under the black banner of his gown the men swept everything before them. But the mob was reinforced, and the " forlorn hope " was again driven into a corner. Out it dashed, though, against the great human barrier which encircled it, but again fell back like a broken wave, collecting its scattered waters as it retired. At that moment a chemist's shop was broken open. The mob seized some bottles. One grazed Reginald's temple.

"Come on !" cried he, " we won't be butchered here," knocking a bargee senseless to the ground.

Once more the little band of heroes charged. This time the mob dispersed like a great cloud pouring down the street. Right on did the cavaliers charge, with Reginald like a second Rupert, leading the van. Through and through did they cut their way.

" Your name and college," cried the proctor,

seizing Reginald's arm, but Reginald not seeing who it was, dashed him to the ground, and on he went, leading the main body, which had just arrived, sweeping the street.

But Reginald Neville was, as we have said, a name known all over Oxford, and the proctor had no difficulty in recognising him. Next morning Reginald was sent for. In vain he pleaded the extenuating circumstances, but the proctor was inexorable.

"I am very sorry for you, Mr. Neville, but I must make an example for once, I will have this sort of thing put down." And so Reginald was then and there expelled.

Reginald rushed back to his rooms. There was a letter upon the table; it was from Minnie, who writes that "dear mamma's grave is still covered with flowers, some of which I have gathered for you."

He took up the letter, and kissed it; tears flowed from his eyes. He had time to think what had happened. Black ruin stared him in the face. All hope gone; all hope of a good degree. What would the angry colonel say? He cared little for him. What would poor Minnie do? He leant his head upon the table, and wept bitterest tears.

Amherst came up.

"Will you go home to my father's, until something can be done?"

But Reginald declined, and now his grief had risen into anger. The news had spread. Within half-an-hour the first dun had arrived. Unlucky dun, to meet Reginald at that inopportune moment! There was not a man in St. Matthew's who was not grieved for Reginald. The very "Dons" interceded for him, but the proctor would not listen.

CHAPTER XVI.

STRUGGLES FOR LIFE.

THE quicksilver of Reginald's spirits rose as suddenly as it had fallen. How beautifully we all build castles in the air! How magnificently, as he went to London by the train, did he furnish his library and drawing-room; no expense, no pains spared! Amherst had promised to forward all Reginald's things, who was not surprised shortly to receive a letter from the colonel, with whom the fellows of St. Matthew's had of course communicated. It was rather severe, but on the whole, kind. Reginald, stung with remorse, determined to carve his own road. The world was his oyster, and with his pen-knife and paper-cutter he would open it: a good number of us in the attempt only succeed in cutting our own hands. He

33—2

wrote to the colonel saying he would relieve
him of his trusteeship. The colonel acceded, and
next week saw Reginald sign the release, and
become possessor of some four hundred pounds,
the amount of his fortune. Why, he owed a
good deal more than that at Oxford. Yet
still his castle did not topple down. By paying
the tradesmen some of them half down, some
of them rather more, he was, for the present,
left undunned.

And what was Reginald's castle, with its gardens,
and acres, and fine woods, and parks? How I
should like to sell by auction one of these fine
castles, which so many of us build, with its spa-
cious rooms and its fine airy situation! On the
strength of it Reginald had already taken lodgings
in the neighbourhood of St. James's-square, at two
guineas a-week. This was not much, certainly, for
the possessor of a castle. To-day he thought he
would dispose of some of his castle, and entered a
fashionable bookseller's with——his poems, for they
were his castle. His poems would of course sell.
He would make money, and thus become famous.

He would marry Minnie, to whom he had not dropped a hint concerning his late misfortune. The colonel would be proud of him. Aston himself would rejoice at his triumph. Such thoughts passed in poor Reginald's mind, as he entered the shop of Messrs. Wordes and Co., Pall Mall. What is Reginald's surprise! Surely Messrs. Wordes and Co. are mad! They actually refuse to cast a glance at his manuscript. Reginald left their shop in disgust, and turned to Messrs. Caxton, in Piccadilly: are they mad too? They assure him they have twenty poets a-day—" a most edifying sign of the times, too," remarks Caxton, junior. Reginald leaves them too, and turns to Messrs. Types, in the Strand. The same result everywhere. The world is overstocked with poets. He went that day into every shop in " the Row." The booksellers fairly knocked down his paper castle, and Reginald that evening was sitting amongst its ruins.

What can he do? Here is Reginald Neville who has spent so much on his education; yet what can he do? He has a splendid museum of clothes, and a small second-hand bootseller's shop. "Shall I hire myself out as a tailor's model?" he asks in bitterness. No, it cannot be; and from the lowest vales he again soars up to the highest mountain peaks. He will write articles for the Magazines. But what shall he write about? What subject does he know? He can't sit down, and manufacture articles, as a thousand steel-springs are made from a piece of iron an inch square. In fact, he knows nothing— knows less than nothing, for he doesn't know just yet that he knows that.

I have read in novels of young gentlemen succeeding in a most miraculous manner in life. Novelists are great magicians. Their heroes surmount all difficulties. One hero have I especially in my mind, who, after being plucked at Oxford, comes up to London, jumps in a moment into the editorial saddle of a newspaper, writes criticisms on public men, theatres, pictures, and what not, besides giving the world a most delightful novel, filled with the most life-like characters, sparkling with wit. But

he had the introduction of a friend. Ah!
happy novelist, and happy hero to have a friend
in need !

But there was in Reginald's case no *Deus ex
machinâ,* no editors wanting leading article writers;
no newspaper proprietors willing, not to say eager,
to buy his contributions; no enterprising booksellers starting rival magazines.

But Reginald was not the man to give up
a thing in despair. He sat down at once to
write an essay, which he found not quite so easy
a matter to do in London. " The roaring of
the wheels," as Mr. Tennyson writes, is not very
favourable to study, but worse than that is the
roaring of the street vendors. Reginald's landlord assures him that it is a very quiet street.
But he must have peculiar notions of quiet-
ness. First of all, early in the morning, as if
to frighten it away, comes an Italian with a
peculiarly energetic organ; he leads the van of
all the noises. No sooner has he commenced
than he is followed by three Jews, one of whom
shouts a long " clo-o-o," the other screams " lo,"

and the other a sharp, quick " O," many times repeated. Then there come screams of new milk and hearth-stones pronounced in a manner no printer can imitate in type, and a boy with water-cresses and cat's-meat, and chimes of muffin-bells, a postman who nearly batters in the door, and finally, a man who growls like one of the beasts in the Zoological Gardens; what he meant Reginald never did discover; and so the chorus of noises goes on all day jangling and wrangling through the streets and the neighbouring squares, as if London had been abandoned to a tribe of the Objibeway Indians.

Reginald's councils of ways and means were every week becoming more numerous; and at one held to-day he determined to leave the aristocratic west for the more plebeian north of London; and evening found him wending his way home with lawyers' clerks to the neighbourhood of Camden Town, where the shops run out from private houses into the street, as if to overthrow the street vendors.

Time was still fast running on with him, and

no employment, though he had made applications at every newspaper office in London, and his purse is not well garrisoned to hold out a long siege. Who would think as he walked down the street, with that good suit of clothes so fashionably made, that in a few weeks he will be penniless? Cabmen are sure he wants a cab, and persist in driving up close to the pavement; they think he has come from the West End simply on an exploring tour, or has lost his way. So he has, but not in London alone, but on the ocean of life: he has left the rest of the fleet, and is sailing without chart or compass.

"What can I do?" is still the question Reginald asks himself, for he must harp upon the same string, which gives a most harsh answer. Had he not once all sorts of plans for the amelioration of the poor and the improvement of the working classes? They might now much more reasonably set up a plan for his improvement. "That little shoe-black aged twelve years, in his red coat, is a far better soldier in this battle of life than I," thought Reginald; "he at all events

can earn his living; but what can I do? Why,
I can write sonnets; can knock off a copy of
Greek Alcaics, can translate a page of Thucy-
dides at sight;" all very creditable, but not very
useful accomplishments in this world as it is
constituted in the nineteenth century, as Reginald finds out to his cost.

Can't he turn schoolmaster and teach these
valuable performances? But schoolmasters must
have degrees, and ushers must not have been
expelled from the university. "Why not advertise in the *Times* for pupils?" So Reginald did,
with about as much success as if he had said
he was open for an engagement as leading-article
writer to that paper. Seriously, what is Reginald to do? Here is Reginald, a full-grown
man, with hands and legs, neither of which is
he able to employ for his own benefit, with three
daily recurring meals, with certain weekly recurring pieces of paper called "bill for lodgings,"
and "bill for washerwoman," and his purse so
light that he has to feel twice for the money
before it appears. He finds he must emigrate

once more : no great harm in rising from a two-pair back to an attic, for he is too proud to write to Amherst for aid, which Amherst would give in a minute without asking, if he did but know Reginald's position.

So he migrated once more, for the sake of cheapness, into an attic in one of those back streets where the shops are of a peculiar order, where the greengrocer sells coals and ginger-beer, and his shop is ornamented with red locks of carrots and a few heartless cabbages—one of those streets which is curiously enough always full of dyers' shops—pity the street itself cannot be renovated—and next to the dyer's a flourishing bone and rag emporium, with its windows glazed with brown paper, and then a barber's shop with its flagless pole, and then a cookshop full of chains of sausages with their fat, greasy links, and the whole street finally finished by a gin-palace and its child the pawnbroker's shop. From his high attic window Reginald now looked down upon vast red prairies of brick and tile, along which by night prowled wild troops of cats, leaping

tiger-like from parapet to parapet. His meals
he was obliged to eat at one of those cheap coffee-
houses, greasy and dark, where the coffee drinks
like boiled Thames-water, and the cold meat
is ever lukewarm with the heat of the room,
and the girl who waits is in a shiny state about
her face with grease and perspiration, where the
freshest newspaper is coffee-stained and blackened
with finger marks, as if it had been read by a
thousand chimney-sweeps.

Reginald, however, still buoyed himself up with
hope. He had two or three articles nearly ready,
which were to be sent off to various magazines,
and would be sure not only to supply the tempo-
rary wants of the day, but open the road for
future operations. There are three letters on
his drawers, which now served him for a writing
desk. Reginald hurriedly breaks their seals; the
first runs as follows:—

" Sir,

"I consider your article ably written, but
do not conceive that the subject would interest

the public at the present moment. For this reason only am I disinclined to avail myself of your kindness.

"Yours obediently,

"W. De Wordes."

The second was a printed circular from the editor of the *Strand Magazine;* the third a note from Reade the great bookseller, precisely similar in meaning to Wordes. These three notes fairly crushed Reginald for a time; and the next post brought a letter from Minnie, giving but a very poor account of little Flo. But still Reginald knew no despair; he set to work with fresh vigour at new articles.

It was burning summer time: Reginald longed for the country, and the trees, and green fields, the song of birds, and running brooks. There was a girl hawking flowers down below; Reginald rushes down, and with his last penny buys a nosegay. A few withered flowers in an attic in London! yet what thoughts do they inspire of blessed haunts where the earliest primroses and violets bloom. Reginald's essay is on the *Midsummer Night's Dream,* and he writes on faster and better as he gazed at them. " Wordes surely won't refuse this for his review," thought Reginald; and he wrote on, forgetting there is a world of want and care around; and at last woke up from his dream, remembering that there was dinner to be bought and no money.

Late on that evening did he pass, when he thought he was unnoticed, into that bank of England around whose tills are so many wretched, haggard customers. He hastily rushed to the nearest coffee-house and devoured dinner, for he had tasted nothing since morning. And that article, what became of it? Here is Wordes' letter:—

" SIR,

" The subject you have chosen is, I fear, too hackneyed to admit of any novelty of treatment; and I beg on that account to return your paper to you.

"Yours obediently,

"W. DE WORDES."

Should he enlist at once? turn actor? invest in a broom and sweep the crossings?' were the thoughts that passed through Reginald's mind; and then, in addition to all these miseries from without, had he none from within? That little attic which he can measure across with his arms is full of a legion of horrid spectres. But Reginald fought them bravely and boldly: he knew that to give up now would be as fatal as to the traveller on the Alps to lie down and sleep. His safety was to keep stirring, however little progress he might make, even though he might go backward.

Summer is past; but Reginald has not seen her: autumn is here; but what calendar has he to go by, except those pawn tickets which he carries about on his person for fear any one should see them at his lodgings, and all the applications from unsatisfied Oxford tradesmen who are now growling at him through the post-office.

"Your articles, sir, are very good, but they are on subjects on which every one fancies he can write," says the editor of the *Strand Maga-*

zine, with whom Reginald made up his mind to have an interview to-day, for he is tired of having articles returned. "If, however, you will write upon some subject about which people don't know, and wish to be informed, and it agrees with my views, I shall be most happy to insert it," he added.

So Reginald goes home once more, and sets to work again with a lighter heart.

CHAPTER XVII.

THE DARKEST HOUR IS THAT BEFORE DAWN.

REGINALD's purse was now always empty, and his only resource the *mont-de-piété*, for he was still too proud to write to any of his Oxford friends to borrow from them, or tell them of his misfortunes. When first he went there, he used to approach the shop by circuitous lanes and alleys. But the skin providentially thickens, and he now would walk in boldly. Yet, somehow or another, he had always the feeling that he was a thief as soon as he entered the shop, —perhaps it was the goods in the place that gave him that feeling. Very wonderful was the collection of Mr. Lazars; and Mr. Lazars himself was equally a curiosity. A little, short man he was, with a bald shiny head, and two pens

on each side of his ears like horns, everlastingly
calculating on the back of tickets to the value
of a farthing. It little mattered what you
brought Mr. Lazars, a casket of pearls or a
coffin, he was determined to lend you the mini-
mum sum. Then he had one or two assistants.
There was the flippant young assistant, who
" chaffed " poverty ; and held up the poor people's
handkerchiefs as the character in the *Nubes* does
the rags of Euripides, with an ὦ Ζεῦ διόττα
expression, whilst another attended to the wooden
pipe. More things went up that pipe than ever
came down. At first Reginald used to go in
at a side door, a sort of private entrance to the
bank, and find himself in a kind of witness-box
or confessional, with other confessionals on each
side of him, where he could hear his neighbours
confessing their poverty. Nearly everything that
Reginald had was pawned. There still remained
a dressing-case, which had belonged to his father.
It must be flung to the devouring monster, Hun-
ger, to appease him. With it under his arm he
emerged from his lodgings late in the evening ;

for he did not wish his landlady to know his errand : for Poverty is, after all, much prouder than her sister, Riches. He reached Mr. Lazars, over whose doorway is written, with needless sarcasm, that he keeps an iron safe for the better security of jewels and valuables.

" Now, sir, what's your business to-day ? " this was Mr. Lazars' usual salutation. Reginald handed him the dressing-case in silence. Mr. Lazars turned the key, tilted the lid, pulled up the tray, opened the bottles, examined the silver stoppers, as if he was a searcher in the Customs' House. " How much on this ? "

" A few sovereigns, say only seven or eight," Reginald replied.

" Can't do it; can't indeed," Lazars returned, in a pathetic voice, as if Reginald was going to ruin him. " It's very old-fashioned; quite out of date; advance you two ten; can't do more; here, Isaacs, make out the ticket; dressing-case, two ten," said he, anticipating Reginald's answer. At that moment a pale, lady-like woman entered, timidly looking round. Lazars' quick eye saw

34—2

her. "Now then, ma'am," said he, putting out his coarse, thick hand, instinctively knowing she had something to give him; for few people came into Lazars' shop late on Saturday night to buy anything, especially poor females in black. She timidly drew back a deep veil, which hid her features, which were very beautiful, though pale and wan; and timidly stretching forth a thin white hand, gave him a miniature, set round with pearls. "What do you want for this?" said Lazars, in his rough way.

Her pale hand rested on the counter to give her support. She had evidently known a better fortune. Her long black hair came undone at that minute; she put her hand up to her face to fasten it back, and when she replaced her hand on the counter, it was wet with tears. Lazars made her some paltry offer.

"No, I cannot part with my poor mother's picture for that; not though I starve," and she went out of the shop; when, suddenly stopping on the door-sill, a thought flashed across her mind, and coming back, she said—"What would

you give me for my long black hair?" shower-
ing it down.

Lazars felt it with his thick hand. Lazars
was a judge of anything, and replied—

" It will depend on how much you have."

She left the shop. Lazars was perfectly un-
moved, and went on checking off some tickets.
Reginald lingered on purpose to see the result.
In a few minutes she returned, bringing her
long hair she had cut off. Lazars put it in the
scales, and advanced some twenty or thirty shil-
lings. The Carthaginian women cut off their
hair to make bowstrings, to defend their country.
Englishwomen sell theirs to save them from
starvation. Reginald walked home saddened,
thinking of poor Miss Garland, wondering what
her fate was in that vast Babylon, gazing in-
quisitively into each passer's face, to see if it
might be her's.

Another three months had passed, and every
day Reginald was poorer. His clothes were all
pawned, books sold—he had nothing left. Starvation stared him in the face. He still hoped

he might soon hear from some of the editors
to whom he had sent contributions, but day after
day passed away, and no reply came. For six
days had he tasted nothing but bread and a little
coffee, which he had procured on credit at a
neighbouring coffee-house. Such a diet soon told
its tale. He began to feel a swelling in his
throat, which gradually increased, becoming more
painful each day, so that if now he had had
anything, he could not have swallowed it. The
next morning he was too weak to rise; for
two days he had absolutely touched nothing;
and now lay too helpless to turn, with his throat
swollen to a fearful size, burning with agony.
He felt himself dying—he fell into a dreamy
doze—he knew nothing—he awoke—there was a
doctor by his bed-side.

"What are you doing here?" asked Reginald,
and too weak to say more, fell back into his
former condition.

In a day or two more he was better.

"There is a letter for you," said his landlady.

He was scarcely strong enough to break the

seal. To his surprise a ten-pound note dropped out. There was nothing else; he turned to the post-mark, which was that of the general-office, and therefore gave no clue. The hand-writing he could not recognise. The sight of the money not only cheered him, but his landlady also, by her arrears of rent being paid.

To-day he is well enough to walk out, and takes his essay, which he finished on the first night of his illness, to the editor of the *Strand Magazine*. It was accepted, but somehow or another, unlike the hero of a popular novel, Reginald came not away jingling the bright sovereigns in his waistcoat pocket. Like other ordinary beings, he had to wait till a few days after the publication, which unluckily did not take place for two months; and then he not only had the pleasure of receiving a cheque, but he can go to the coffee-houses and reading-rooms, and see the people take up the *Strand Magazine*, and watch them if they turn to his article; and then, too, look through all the papers to see the notices of it, which are all favourable, so that his essay is quite a hit, and Bellafont gives him another commission.

Work now comes, but still very slowly; no slashing leading articles, such as your hero writes. Reginald must do exactly what the editor, who is also publisher, tells him. To-day he has a bundle of manuscripts of the seventeenth century to be deciphered. He is astonished when Reginald reads them off fluently, for he had had so much practice in the old library at Merepool. Reginald takes them to his lodgings, and works all day, and at night strolls down to some dining-rooms in the Strand, and knows the pleasure of paying with the money he had earned.

" The evening paper, sir," said the waiter.

Reginald seized it, for he knew the Oxford class list was out that day, and there was Amherst in the first class. He involuntarily gave a cheer, which made his neighbours look round.

And at Bushwood, what was going on there? Lord Cokeborough was still as frequent in his visits as before, and closeted with Aston for a longer time than ever.

"That is agreed upon, then, my lord," said Aston, giving him a bundle of papers.

They contained Minnie's death-warrant. Lord Cokeborough made little reply. In the evening Aston sent for his daughter. He hardly knew how to open the proceedings, but kept rapping his ivory paper-knife on a Parliamentary blue-book before him.

"Yes, papa, I have come."

"I have sent for you," at last he said, "to tell you that the arrangements for your marriage with Lord Cokeborough are settled."

Minnie seldom became angry, but if anything could vex her, it was this one subject; she, however, suppressed her feelings, though her flashing eye and her hectic face told the struggle within.

"Oh, papa, you surely think you are in France, where the parents always make their children's marriages!" she said, with a smile, hoping thus to ward him off.

"Lord Cokeborough will himself call tomorrow."

"Well, papa, I am very much obliged to you

for the information—forewarned is forearmed, you know."

"And you will at once consent to his proposal?"

"Lord Cokeborough, if a gentleman, as I take him to be, will wish me to consent to nothing against my feelings; and if, as you have often said, he is really attached to me, nothing will please him so much as what pleases me," she answered, with some warmth, but still calmly.

"If Lord Cokeborough cannot persuade you, I command you to marry him."

"Command," said Minnie, bitterly, "command," pausing on the word; "and will you command me against poor mamma's dying wish, against the last words she ever breathed? No, I am sure you won't, papa!" and she clasped him round the neck; but Aston was proof,—he shook his daughter off.

"Remember, Lord Cokeborough will call to-morrow."

Minnie now became somewhat angry.

"Am I to be bought and sold, then, like a sheep

in the market, to the highest bidder?" and she rushed away weeping to her own room.

The next morning Lord Cokeborough called. Minnie did not wish openly to disobey her father, but at the same time determined she would never marry any one but Reginald.

"I think, Lord Cokeborough, you might, if only for the sake of decency, have waited a few months longer," she said, pointing to her mourning dress, which she still wore.

Lord Cokeborough felt the reproof.

"I hardly think too, this is a time for you and my father to be talking of marriage, and giving in marriage, when my sister Florence is lying at death's door in the house."

Lord Cokeborough, who had expected no resistance, was completely taken aback by this line of defence, as it admitted of no attack. He apologized as well as he could, and Minnie was thus left for a time mistress of the situation.

CHAPTER XVIII.

THE LAST.

BELLAFONT, who, as we have said, was editor as well as publisher of the *Strand Magazine*, kept his contributors together by means of a *soirée* every now and then; and by-and-by Reginald received an invitation to his house in Cambridge Terrace. Bellafont had once been an errand boy, and on "Magazine day" carried about the Review which he now edited. Bellafont knew the public taste, and the Magazine, in his hands, had largely increased in circulation; Bellafont, too, knew well the value of money, which is more than some of his contributors did. His house in Cambridge Terrace, if not in the best style, was substantially furnished. Somewhere about eight o'clock did Reginald knock at the door. A servant seemed to

spring to it, and in a moment he was ushered into
a small room, where Mrs. Bellafont and the eldest
Miss Bellafont were making tea. Mrs. Bellafont
had been instructed by her husband as to the
various contributors who were invited, and their
various productions in the last number of the Review; but Mrs. Bellafont, not being particularly
literary, had quickly forgotten her lesson; and as
soon as Reginald's name was announced, began
complimenting him on a most learned archæo-
logical paper written by the famous antiquarian
Mr. Stone. Mrs. Bellafont was a little thick, low,
pollard sort of woman, whom nature, in her early
years, had cut down in her growth, and from the
effects of which she seemed never to have re-
covered. Mrs. Bellafont was a grocer's daughter,
and her tea was always excellent. The little
woman to-night was decked in all her finery to do
honour to the occasion. Round her wrists twined
two bracelets, which looked very much like golden
handcuffs; and her hands were covered with
rings, which lay perfectly imbedded in her little
fat fingers. Miss Bellafont quite rivalled, if not

surpassed her mother; round her wrists coiled two
fierce golden snakes with terrible eyes and stings,
whilst on her breast nestled an aspic, as if sleeping
on some Cleopatra's breast.   Why are women so
fond of such horrible reptiles?   The old serpent
that tempted Eve seems still to possess some terrible fascination over modern ladies.   They might
as well wear toads and frogs at once; the former
would assuredly be more in keeping, for a certain
great poet tells us that it "wears a precious jewel
on its head."   Miss Bellafont and Reginald tried to
raise a feeble conversation, but it soon altogether
dwindled away, and he sipped his tea in silence,
and was presently conducted to the drawing-room
by Bellafont's servant, who had been lately put into
livery, with the Bellafont crest on the buttons,
stuck all about his coat like spangles.   Some
twenty people were in the room, all strangers to
Reginald, to some of whom Bellafont introduced
him.   Copies of the *Strand Magazine* were lying
on the table, as well as a number of its rival, the
Temple Review, and their respective merits were
being canvassed, much to the disparagement of the

latter, which was published by Bellafont's great opponent, Mr. Types, in Fleet Street. A number of newspapers, all with favourable criticisms on the *Strand Magazine*, were scattered about.

" Your paper is very favourably noticed, Mr. Neville," said Bellafont; " look here," and he handed him the *St. Stephen's Herald*, the *Westminster News*, and other papers. Reginald had seen them all before, but it was a double pleasure to read the notices with Bellafont standing by his side. Bellafont is always terribly fidgety about his Magazine; but all the newspapers had pronounced the present number as the best which had ever been issued, so that Bellafont was in high spirits. The current number of the *Temple Review* happened to be very poor; perhaps this had something to do with Bellafont's good humour.

And now, perhaps, the reader will expect me to give a long and precise account of the great literary celebrities to-night at Bellafont's. I think if some of the publishers, when they give a literary dinner, would but advertise the fact in the *Times*, and that tickets for admission to see the lions fed, after the Zoological Gardens fashion, could be obtained for ten guineas, they would realize enough to pay for their butcher's and wine merchant's bills for the next twenty years.   But if the reader will believe me, I can assure him there was nothing very different about the twenty people there, from any other twenty people assembled in any other room.   The twenty gentlemen talked about as much nonsense as any other twenty gentlemen: the ladies were as charming as most ladies are, and had as good appetites as most ladies have at supper.   There were no very profound or very brilliant remarks. Still out of twenty or thirty people, there must always be some two or three remarkable, if not by genius, by appearance, or for some other reason, which was the case here.   There was Mr. Stone, the great archæologist, resurrectionist, gravedigger, and what not.   Mr. Stone had, with deciphering almost illegible inscriptions, so injured his eyes, that one of the wits of the *Strand Magazine* said he had become stone-blind.   Mr. Stone was a man considerably past his youth, if ever he had known such a period of existence, and had recently married a very young and pretty little wife. She is sitting on the sofa picking her fan to pieces, and talking to Miss Bayes, a young lady who has lately published a volume of poems, which was so severely cut up in the *Temple Review*. Mrs. Stone is excessively pretty, and has nice black hair, which she dresses in good taste, is fond of balls and theatres, to all which things Stone has the greatest aversion. Stone would rather sit in the pillory for a day, than listen for an hour to the piano. The consequence of all this is, that there are all sorts of stories about Mr. and Mrs. Stone, how Stone makes his little wife the whole day through copy old dull deeds and rolls and manuscript; but quarrels are not alone peculiar to the literary world. Poor little Mrs. Stone! she might as well have married Euclid, or Sir Isaac Newton, or Copernicus, or Copernicus's system; but unhappy marriages are not uncommon elsewhere besides in the literary world. Then there was Miss Bayes, who when Reginald was introduced to her, without the least provocation on his part, rushed off into a florid discourse, how she should like to dwell in

the savannahs and the wild woods of some wild
country, all alone with the flowers and the wild
beasts ; and having exhausted this topic, darted off
into a rhapsody upon Shelley, and natural religion,
and metaphysics, and the rights of women, and
the superiority of the negroes over the whites, on
all which subjects she possessed equal knowledge.
Then there was the great Mr. Goswell, who had
lately published a most abstruse work on philo-
sophy in fifty volumes quarto, which none of the
critics could understand, and therefore abused.
Mr. Goswell, it is said—but I do not relate the fact
from my own knowledge—reads twenty hours a-
day, is obliged to drink steel and quinine at dinner
to keep up his system, and takes a constitutional
up and down the passage of his house whilst he
swallows his tea. Like Stone he has long lost his
sight, and always reads with his nose. But I must
not say more, or else I shall be accused of making
all sorts of revelations, and shall never be asked to
Bellafont's again. And I therefore implore the
reader, if he should hear that any literary gentleman is short-sighted, or reads twenty hours a-day,

or is not on the best terms with his wife, or that any literary lady has lately published a volume of poems, which in all probability has been most deservedly cut up, not to associate them with Mr. and Mrs. Stone, or Miss Bayes, or Mr. Goswell, for I should blush to betray any of the secrets of the literary world, which have been entrusted to me in the strictest confidence. So the reader must, for the present, be content. All I can now say is, that Bellafont gives a capital supper, with some of his best wine—and Bellafont has as good a cellar as any man alive—and that Reginald contrived to sit next pretty little Mrs. Stone, who, though well educated, is not a literary person, and therefore perhaps one of the most agreeable in the room, that he gives her his arm downstairs to the cab, and immediately after walked back to his lodgings.

Reginald's connection now fast increased. Bellafont gave him an introduction to the *St. Stephen's Herald*, upon which he obtained regular employment. For the first time, for above a year, he got out into the country upon a Sunday. It was summer. Bright flowers were bursting, like sweetest

thoughts, from the teaming brain of earth; the
stream glided by like some azure and golden snake
coiling along the grass; the heavens swam above
like some vast blue ocean, in which clouds floated
like lazy pinnaces, with their white sails half furled.
He lay down on a bank, and mused on the past
eighteen months. Into that small space had been
crowded the events of many ordinary years.

Reginald had long since been able to emerge
from that sewer of a street, and change to healthier
quarters. He had gone where so many men of
letters congregate, into that half College, half
lodging-house, semi-Bohemia, the Temple. Oppo-
site to him were Amherst's rooms, with his name
painted over the door, as in old College days, who
was now reading for the *Bar*. They again, as in
old days, used to breakfast together; and old faces
would congregate again in the evening by Reginald's fireside.

Letters often came from Minnie, giving but a
poor account of little Flo. Her face had now a
hectic flush on it, like the red spot which Reginald
and Minnie used to see in the woods on those trees

which were marked to be cut down. At last comes the fatal note, still wet with its writer's tears. One more orphan child has found its mother in heaven!

A week after, as Reginald is sitting in his room writing, some one rushes in. It is Minnie, pale and haggard.

"Dear Flo's funeral took place yesterday, we buried her next dear mamma." This is all the poor girl can say. She loved her mother, and her mother was gone; she loved Flo, and Flo too was taken away: "I have no one else to love now but you, Reginald, and to you have I come," cried the poor girl, sobbing bitterly against his breast. She had been tried in sorrow's hottest furnace.

That evening Mr. Aston Neville himself appeared. His countenance, and his hair, which now was gray, testified that he too had suffered. The film had fallen from his eyes; he now saw that gold, and Burke's *Peerage* and *Baronetage* itself, do not weigh much in the scales of life against true love and contentment. Reginald could not help pitying him; he had lost his wife, had lost his daughter, and now would lose his only child unless she would return. Reginald felt he had been too severe upon him at his wife's death.

"Yes, obey my poor wife's commands, only, only come back to me, Minnie," sobbed the broken-hearted father. It was a piteous spectacle.

"Forgive! forgive! who shall cast the first stone?" thought Reginald to himself, and went up and took Aston's hand, and pressed it silently.

And now let us conclude, and like those dear old stories we read when we were children, finish happily. Minnie and Reginald were married some six months after, but not till the old church at Bushwood was restored. They paused as they went in and as they came out by Mrs. Neville's and little Flo's graves, which were now covered with flowers; and the second time Minnie whispered to Reginald, "We have now obeyed dear mamma's wishes."

And Lord Cokeborough? If you were a constant reader of the *Morning Plush*, you would have known that he soon afterwards married Miss Higgins, the great Manchester cotton-spinner's daughter, and in the same paper you might have read a description of Miss Ancaster's dress when she married the gallant Saber. Colonel Ancaster still lives at Merepool Abbey in Fentonshire the Blest, and still believes in his old Tory creeds. But let us not blame him or anybody else. It is the same wind that drives one vessel due east, and another southward. And Lady Mary? She still has as great an aversion as ever to handsome governesses; and ill-natured people say that it is her ladyship who is constantly advertising in the *Times* for that most remarkable commodity, " a good plain governess."

And what about all the other actors and actresses in this history? Amherst is a rising barrister, and has come down with " the jolly governor" several times to Bushwood, and " the jolly governor " was jollier than ever, and made Minnie for the first time laugh as she used long ago. And good old Mr. Golding? he is still alive, and there is now no necessity for his subscribing to the Bushwood Schools. And Miss Golding? Why, Reginald's wife wants Amherst to marry her. And Mr. Benison? Aston lately offered him Bushwood Church, but he refused to leave his poor desolate flock at Stoke Furnace, and still toils amongst its fetid bylanes and alleys.

One person is there yet? poor Miss Garland, where is she? One evening, when Reginald was engaged upon the *St. Stephen's Herald*, he went as theatrical critic to witness the *début* of Mrs. G——. She was no other than Miss Garland, who had taken to the stage as a profession, and there married. "I did not write, because I thought that you, like all the world, would consider my profession as a disgrace," she said, when he met her at the stage door; "but what else was I to do? no other avenue, no other means of obtaining an honest livelihood." Reginald knew then who it was had sent him the ten-pound note. She had seen him in the street, followed him to his lodgings, and there made inquiries of the landlady, whose confidence she gained. And Miss Garland is a visitor whenever she pleases at Bushwood.

And here to-day has Mr. Aston Neville come to

tell Reginald of his intention to resign for Stoke Furnace, and Reginald is in the midst of electioneering business. One life has just closed, another is opening — the highest, perhaps, that a man can aspire to, that of governing, or rather helping his fellow-creatures to govern themselves, to aid God, as it were, in developing a perfect moral law, so that justice be done both to Him and all of us his creatures.

THE END.